# NERO

## BOOK 1:
## THE BEAST EMERGES

## Christofer Nigro

**Cover Logo Design and Formatting by Elden Ardiente of Lungga Creatives (https://www.facebook.com/lunggacreative)**

**The Jack Dog created by Charles Hejna**

# DEDICATIONS

The first chronological book in the saga of Mike Nero (later to become known as Beowolf, once he finally reaches the status of hero and monster hunter) is lovingly dedicated to the memory of my amazing grandmother Gertrude "Trudie" Nigro. As I type these words circa October 2020 it has been almost a year since she left us at the ripe old age of 95, and our family was truly blessed to have had her in our lives for so many years. I will never forget all she has done for me and the many fun afternoons we spent watching horror movies together. We did not always see eye to eye, but no one in my life had ever loved me more despite our differences, and there has been no one I loved more than her. I will continue to work hard to make her proud and to accomplish all she believed that I could!

I also dedicate this initial work and the continuing saga of Nero to the many great authors, artists, actors, directors, and video game developers who contributed to werewolf fiction throughout the many decades that helped create my lifelong fascination with this coolest of all monsters. Thank you in particular to actors Lon Chaney Jr. and Paul Naschy for famously and expertly bringing the tragic but poignant characters of Larry Talbot (a.k.a., The Wolf Man) and Waldemar Daninsky (a.k.a., El Hombre Lobo, the Wolf Man of Spain) to life on the silver screen; author Guy Endore for writing *The Werewolf of Paris*, which went a long way towards bringing the werewolf to literature in the 20th century; author Stephen King for writing *The Cycle of the Werewolf* and giving these amazing monstrosities some truly great legitimacy in more modern literature; author/artist Richard Corben for his many amazing werewolf stories in the comic book format that are a wonder to behold; the creative crews behind great werewolf flicks like *The Howling* and *An American Werewolf in London* that fascinated horror fans of my generation; and the many writers and artists who brought us several decades of great comic book stories featuring Jack Russell, the titular *Werewolf by Night* of Marvel Comics, who showed us that lycanthropes can not only sustain a series as continuing characters, but can be heroes and protectors instead of just scary monsters that end the lives of any person that crosses their paths. The creative inspiration given to me from all of you and too many more to mention has been valuable beyond words to describe!

Finally, this dedication would not be complete without the inclusion of shout-outs to my childhood friends Charles and John Hejna, the former of whom created the story of the terrifying Jack Dog back in the day (which was built around an actual scary-*looking* dog that dwelled in a house right around the corner from Charlie and John during those years), a monstrous canine which makes his debut published appearance in this very tome. I had a lot of great times with the two youngest Hejna siblings, we wrought a lot of memorable mischief together in the neighborhood we shared back then that had much influence on building my creative imagination, and in some ways made Wild Hunt Press possible. I am proud to have re-established contact with Charlie and John a few years back, where we discuss the nostalgic memories of the days when we terrorized the 'hood and created cool stories about things that go bump in the night like the Jack Dog. And I haven't even mentioned the Witch Sisters yet, another creation of Charlie's that will receive their much-deserved literary debut in an upcoming Wild Hunt title (but are referenced in this very novella). Thank you for those great times, guys!

# NERO

## BOOK 1:
## THE BEAST EMERGES

*Buffalo, New York*
*October, shortly before Halloween 1981*

When I started 8<sup>th</sup> grade last month here at Woodlawn Magnet School, it was supposed to be a new beginning for me. That's what I thought; that's what I hoped. It was supposed to be a real difference from the bad old days at that Catholic dungeon of a parochial school known and hated across the breadth of Buffalo as Holy Apostate. I was as thankful as a flea in fur when the school was closed, and I had to go elsewhere for my final year of elementary school.

I would finally be away from the bullying faces and fists of both my fellow students and the teachers. In particular I would be away from that jock asshole Dean O'Sullivan, who seemed to hate me more than anyone else I had ever met, and for no reason he ever bothered to explain to me. He was too busy calling me things like "faggot," "fairy," and "cock smoker" to have the time to explain what the hell his problem with me was. And then there was the principal, that bitch Sister Jasmine, who the less I reminisce about the better.

Well, the new beginning here at Woodlawn soon turned out to be more of the same. Most of my peerage took an instant dislike to me. I mean, I get that I would never win a personality contest, nor would I even get nominated for class chalkboard cleaner, but am I really that bad? Maybe it's best I don't ask myself that question. The only friend I've made so far is fellow outcast Greydon Minter, and it figures he's practically the only other kid there as disliked as I am. Our friendship sure as hell isn't doing either of us any favors in the reputation department, but give us a break – we're pretty much all the other has here, even if we do want to kick the shit out of each other almost as often as the other kids do.

My thoughts were rudely interrupted when a dark, steel-strong hand grasped me by the collar as I turned the corridor while running to avoid being late for my second period physical science class. I knew whose hand that was right away, and the deep thundering voice that followed was the final terrifying confirmation.

"Why are you running in the hallways, young man?" the principal Mr. Johnson screamed at me while pushing me up against a wall. "You know there is no running permitted in these halls!"

Trying not to shit myself, I replied, "Sorry, sir, Mr. Johnson, sir. I just didn't want to be late…"

My pathetic apology was also cut off when the principal whacked me hard in the ass as punishment and pushed me in the direction of my next class. "No excuses for that behavior! Now get to class and don't let me catch you running in the halls again!"

Just my luck he had to whack me one like that right in front of at least eight other sneering students. And just my luck those faces had to include the tall, red-haired Maddy Mainfield, whom I had a crush of epic proportions on. She tried not to laugh at my situation, but when Al Jenning pointed and started on me about it, she couldn't help going into giggle mode.

"You're such a spazz, Nero," he said. "I wish Mr. Johnson could just pay me to kick your ass."

"You just want the opportunity to touch my butt," I replied, invoking the mass homophobia popular in the day.

Maddy giggled again as Al, much taller than me and more athletic besides, walked over and pushed me against the wall. He made a fist and cocked it back in a threatening manner. Despite being rather thin back then, I was no slouch in the strength department, having grown up on the mean streets of the Queen City's West Side. But Al was even less of a slouch than I was, and despite pushing back I just couldn't extricate myself from his grip.

"Hit 'im, Al!" David Conroy said as he ran to his friend's side. "Dog his faggot ass!"

As I pushed back harder, Al responded by unexpectedly driving his kneecap into my balls. I buckled over and slid to the floor with my hands covering my aching testicles.

"Whoa," was all Maddy said with a slight smile as David began laughing like a hyena in heat.

I think watching my crush see me humiliated like that by a guy of superior strength and popularity was worse than getting ramrodded in the groin. Well, almost.

"What's going on out here?" we heard the voice of Mrs. Linsky the math teacher say. "Why aren't you people in class?"

"We were on our way there, Mrs. Linsky," Al muttered, "but Nero was acting like a jerk after Mr. Johnson hit him for running in the halls. So, I had to defend myself."

"Mike Nero!" the teacher yelled. "What did I tell you about your behavior?"

"That it's not up to your heavy standards, Mrs. Linksy?" I quipped as I struggled against the searing pain between my legs to get back to my feet.

"You're not funny!" the skinny young teacher with the short hairdo hollered. "You shouldn't be surprised that the other kids get so disgusted with you all the time! Now get to class before I escort you to the office personally."

Not willing to push my luck any further with either peer or official authority figure, I pulled myself to my feet, picked up my bag of books, and scrambled to physical science class without uttering another word. No doubt Mr. Napolsky was missing my hated presence as I was due to fail his latest quiz on the Periodic Table.

Yep, being at WMS was like enjoying the company of Dean O'Sullivan and his many cronies at Holy Apostate all over again. My life was going to be no different here at Woodlawn, and all I could do was hope and pray to *some* deity, any one of them from any pantheon who may have been willing to listen and grant me the means to fight back.

Little did I know my desperate prayers would soon be answered, and in a manner most horrific to anyone who had ever crossed me – and ultimately, in a way that would taint my soul with coal black darkness. The path it ultimately led me to was most interesting, but the long road to get there would be crooked and fraught with pain and trauma.

*\*\*\**

"I wish I had the power to fight back against those assholes!" I whined to my sometimes-good-friend Greydon Minter on the school bus (we called it "The Cheese") while on the way home.

"You and me both, dude," he said as he glanced at the book I was reading: *The Tragedy of Lawrence Talbot* by Lady Jane Ainsley and Anton Zarnak. "You better not let the dickheads at school see you reading that shit. They give you a hard enough time for the comic books as it is."

4

"The life story of this Talbot guy really compels me," I said in response. "The gift of lycanthropy gave him some serious power!"

"Gift? According to what I saw in the movie version, he considered it more of a curse."

I scoffed. "Only because he had no idea what he had, and what he could do with it if he had gotten control over the beast when it emerged. Probably because he grew up a respected kid that had no serious need to defend himself on a regular basis."

"Well, that's all fake shit from those old ass movies anyways."

"Rumor has it that they're based on actual occurrences but passed off as lurid fiction in horror flicks and comic book adaptations."

"Now I'm starting to think you're crazy too!"

"Think whatever you want. People whom the world thinks are crazy have tended to go far in life. 'Crazy' is just their derogatory word for ambition and refusing to conform."

Greydon shook his head. "Whatever, man. But it's funny how you mention all of that, considering that guy who just opened up a little shop a few blocks from me."

Suddenly, I felt my entire body tightening up in surprise as I turned to Greydon. "What guy, and what kind of shop?" I demanded to know.

"Calm down, dude, it's not like it's some model selling naked pictures of herself. It's this weird German-sounding guy called Rutger. Or, maybe he's French? But whatever he is, he operates some type of strange novelty shop where he sells shit like spell books, wolf hide, animal blood and bones, all sorts of herbs, ostrich feathers... and even weirder shit."

"I need to meet him. Today."

"With all the homework Mrs. Kilada assigned us this weekend? I'm lucky if I'll have time for any dinner over the next two days, let alone—"

*"Today.* I'll *pay* you if you show me where that shop is."

Greydon went quiet for a second. "Okay. Maybe the homework can wait since I got all weekend to do it. Or, I can do it Monday morning before leaving for school and on The Cheese going there, like I usually do."

Yea, life was about to change. Drastically. Not just for me, and not just for the status quo of Woodlawn Magnet School, either... the Queen City itself was about to enter a shitstorm.

\*\*\*

I must say that Rutger's shop looked even stranger than Greydon let on. As in, *seriously* strange. It's really hard to describe, but somehow even the architecture of the place seemed, well, just *off* in some way that's difficult to put into words. As if it was built to a sense of aesthetics that was very much outside the norm of human preference. It did seem constructed of wood and mortar like you would expect, but the door of the front entrance was shaped to resemble a sort of circular portal instead of a typical rectangle. Weird.

I was staring at it with a combination of awe and discomfort while Greydon pulled on my sleeve to nag me about the payment I promised him.

"Can't you just give me half today? You aren't paying me too much as it is, so asking for half is, like, not asking for much at all."

"I'll see what I can come up with today, alright?" I replied while swatting his hand away, never taking my eyes off Rutger's bizarro storefront. "And not paying you much? That's an entire week's lunch money, so it's a lot for me!"

"Hey, don't blame me. Blame Reagan for fucking over the economy since he started office."

"Let's just go in, okay? I'm still gonna have to pay this Rutger guy whatever he wants for whatever I might need to get, and I won't be able to get a lot as it is."

"You don't even know what you're gonna need yet!"

"Let's just go in and ask, alright? It's starting to get cold out here. This is Buffalo in October, not Burbank!"

We opened the doors and stepped in to Rutger's shop. As expected, this place was a real trip! What looked like animal skulls – including a few resembling no animal I could recognize – decorated the brightly painted shelves. One section of the small shop was festooned with fat dusty books, some of which looked hundreds of years old (or maybe he just never bothered to clean the place?). There were glass jars and vials filled with various colored liquids, including red fluid that I can only guess was some type of animal blood (because it couldn't be human, right?); one contained a yellowish liquid that I swear to God looked like it must have been... well, I didn't want to say it.

"Is that jar filled with piss?" Okay, Greydon said it, so I didn't have to.

"Um, I dunno. Why don't you take a sip and see if it tastes familiar, dude?"

"No need for that, boys," came a deep voice with a slight Balkan accent from the shadows of a small room to the left of the front desk. "Since if you do that, then I'm afraid you will have to purchase the entire jar. And I can simply answer your question. It is indeed coyote urine, which is good for a variety of spells and potions. I can assure you that it is a top seller here among the practitioners of the mystic arts."

We turned to see who must have been Rutger himself emerge from the darkened entrance to a room located outside the main section of the shop. He was even taller than Greydon (who is 6'6"), thin but well-built in the muscle department. His tan face had worn, parchment-like skin, flat hazel eyes, and thinly cropped copper-colored hair with gray at the temples. His body looked much younger than that face, like no more than mid-30s. The man's teeth were yellow and crooked; and as he got closer, we could see that his fingernails were unusually sharp for a man, with thick callouses visible on his fingertips.

The man was dressed in a gray vest worn over a brown shirt, with faded jeans that were held on by a tied rope rather than a regular belt with a buckle. His feet were covered by dingy shoes that looked as if he had purchased them sometime in the past century. Around his neck was a gleaming necklace in the image of a golden dog or wolf's head baring its teeth in a menacing way. The newness and shine of that medallion seemed a major contrast to the old-looking attire that covered the rest of his body.

"Mike, meet Rutger," Greydon said as if he was introducing me to no one more unusual than his grandmother.

"Nice to meet you," I muttered with a slight gulp as I forced myself to extend my hand to the strange curio shop proprietor.

"My pleasure, Michael," he said as he took my hand in a painfully tight grip and shook it.

I noted that the skin of his palm and fingers felt like sandpaper, and his nails looked even sharper close-up. I tried and failed not to wince as he grasped my hand. And I swear I felt something like a quick surge of electricity exchanged between myself and his necklace – just think of a slightly more powerful version of what you feel when you touch a doorknob and your body loses an electron to get the idea.

"I have been awaiting your visit," the strange guy continued. "Eagerly."

"Um, you have?" I replied in squeamish confusion.

"Indeed." Rutger smiled widely, as if showing off his mouthful of uneven teeth.

"But how is that possible?" I asked.

"Let us just say that this shop serves a purpose here beyond the simple profiting by selling difficult-to-acquire curiosities," Rutger explained. "An additional, non-advertised purpose is to locate young individuals like yourself who have the potential to become distinguished members of the Brotherhood of Fenris."

"The who?" Greydon enquired.

"Fenris, or Fenrir, is the big bad wolf of Norse mythology," I answered, always proud to show off how much I read and studied in my quest to be a writer. "He's one of the three offspring of Loki, the Norse god of mischief, and a giantess lover of his."

"That is correct, Michael!" Rutger said with zeal. The odd man then gave Greydon an intense glare, and my friend turned and walked toward the front of the store with not a single comment. I thought that was very strange, but I was too engrossed by the strange man's continuing spiel to react to it. "Fenris is who we worship. Fenris is who gives us our power. And Fenris can give you the power that you seek as well. Is power not what you are here to acquire?"

At first, my face took on an astonished expression. This bizarre guy seemed to know me better than I knew myself. Was it really just a big coincidence that Greydon found out about this place and told me about it? Or, was he just a pawn in the arms of Fate – maybe I should say the Norns, to put a Norse context to it – being used like a puppet in a performance to guide me here? That was too big to wrap my thoughts around at the moment, though. What I was most interested in was the *power* that Rutger mentioned was mine for the taking, and that a Norse wolf deity could somehow provide it for me.

But what if he was just some weirdo bullshitter? What if Greydon gave him just enough info so they could pull some dumbass joke on me? That's certainly something Greydon would do. But... somehow I just *knew* this guy is on the level, even if I couldn't quite grasp what type of level that might be. It was also as if if that necklace of his had something to do with convincing me of his validity, though to this day I can't really explain how in words.

*Okay, so if he was legit, then what if I can't afford to pay for everything I needed to get the power from Fenris? The price of entry into this Brotherhood of Fenris must cost way too much for a kid like me to come up with. Maybe a payment plan of some sort is possible?*

"Yea, I'm totally down for it," I answered matter-of-factly. "I'm tired of being powerless and at the mercy of every asshole in the world. What do I need to buy or do to get this power?"

"I can simply give you all you need right in this very shop," Rutger said. "Along with a scroll of instructions that will tell you what you need to do with the provided items, and when, and under what set of conditions."

"Okay," I replied with some excitement. "But what kind of power are we talking about here?"

"Nothing less than the power of the *loup garou,* as the French call it. You know what that is, do you not?"

I know I heard him right. But I couldn't have. "You mean… I will gain the power to become a *werewolf?"*

*"Ja,* that is the preferred name to us Germans, at least if we are describing it with your English."

"But, wait… I've read about such creatures before! And…"

"What you mean, young sir, is that you have always been fascinated by them. With the power they have, which is sufficient to reverse the odds against nearly any form of opposition you may encounter in the human world. To safeguard you from fear of any other person. To acquire justice, revenge, entitlement, and to take back anything that may have been taken from you. For that power would be nothing less than the blessing of Fenris, which would come replete with his formidable ferocity, and the physical might of the animal whose form he wears."

"Wow," I said. "That's… quite a way of putting it. I'm totally sold!"

"I was confident you would be," Rutger said with an ominously pleased tone.

I looked over at Greydon to see what he may have had to say about this. It was then I noticed that since Rutger gave him the intense glare a few minutes ago, my best/only friend was off in the corner of the shop, his eyes transfixed on some exotic looking gem kept under a glass case.

9

It was almost like he was in a type of trance, as if it were intended to keep his interest on something unrelated to my visit so he would not be privy to the later segment of my conversation with Rutger.

Something then told me it may not be the best idea for him to hang around here much longer. So, I resolved to complete this too-good-to-be-true-sounding transaction and see if there was any merit to it.

"Okay, speaking of 'sold,' how much is all of this going to cost me? A lot, I imagine, right?"

"Oh, *ja.* The cost of a gift like this does not come cheap and will indeed be *very* high."

*Wonderful.* "Before I ask how much, I'd like to know if a payment plan is possible. I mean, could someone actually put a jar of coyote piss on layaway here?"

"Indeed, there is such a plan," Rutger assured me with a sinister smile. "In fact, you shall have *years* to pay this off. All you need do is take the items I will give you, use them as the included scroll instructs, and you will receive the power of Fenris. Then, you may use that power any way you wish, to acquire anything you want. For *years.* You will gain valuable knowledge and gradually increasing ability based on the experiences you will doubtless bring upon yourself during that span of time.

"Then, years in the future, when the Brotherhood of Fenris comes calling for you, you shall join us in our mission, add your power to the brothers and sisters you shall meet there, with no qualms on your part. That, and that alone, is the price I am charging you for this rare and tremendous gift. I ask for no money, but simply your *loyalty.*"

"Um, okay. But, what exactly is the mission of this Brotherhood that I'll have to get involved with somewhere down the line?"

"That I cannot divulge at this time. But why concern yourself with that at present? When one purchases the radio he has always desired on credit, does he concern himself overly much with the day the debt will come due? *Nein,* he enjoys the benefits provided from said device and worries about crossing the bridge of debt only when the time comes.

"As of now, think of what you will acquire, the years you have to use it as you will, and the fact that you will retain it for the rest of your life. Also keep in mind that when payment comes due, the Brotherhood of Fenris is a powerful lot, so joining that sacred fraternity is hardly a price one should shy away from. Are you afraid to grasp the glory and respect that the world has ever denied you, Michael Nero?"

*He knows my last name too! Did Greydon maybe tell him? If he was actually expecting me, then how did he know about me in the first place?*

"I'm… not afraid. I don't want to be afraid ever again. If I have to live in a world like this, I'd rather do it with the power of Fenris than without it; I'd rather be *somebody* than be stuck on the lowest rung of society for a single day longer, let alone the rest of my life. You have a deal, Rutger."

"Hah! Splendid, young Michael! You shall not regret this decision. Once you conduct the ritual and gain the power, the regrets will from then on be limited to those who dare to cross you."

*Yes! Of course, Greydon was now entranced by that jewelry, so he isn't around to offer his opinion on whether or not I may be making a deal with the Devil. And what if I am? Well, what has the Devil's opposite number, God, ever done for me? Look how his followers treated me at that fucking Catholic school. Look at how that Catholic family of mine thinks of me. If the Devil actually cares, while God obviously doesn't, then* fuck *God and this world he created.*

So, Rutger gathered the stuff I needed with impressive quickness, as if he had the items mostly prepared already. More weirdness.

"In this bag," he explained, "is a belt of wolf hide, two vials of wolf blood, a careful oily tincture of specially mixed herbs, a pendant you will require, and a scroll with both instructions and verses that must be recited at the time indicated… and a few extra items thrown in as, you might say, a bonus. This recitation must be performed with the most sincere of convictions and strongest of emotions. Fenris will only give you this gift of power if you *truly want* to let him into your material form and your soul. If so, then you will become far more than a mortal man. If not, then you will be fated to continue living as you are now, for only those with stern conviction and unrestrained ambition can make use of the potential you possess."

"I get you, man. I gotta ask, though: How many others in Buffalo are you going to lure, or whatever you call it, over to you to receive this offer?"

"That I am also unable to divulge. Know, however, that you are one of but a select few with the proper combination of genetics, spiritual ancestry, natural rapport with the forces from beyond, and personality

11

traits that make you of the proper emotional state of mind to willingly become what you will soon become."

Rutger then handed me a tightly wrapped cloth satchel. "Here is your bag of required items. Take it, follow the instructions in the scroll I included to the very letter, and do not come back here under any circumstances. We will meet again, but not for years hence. May the glory of Fenris and the might of his paternal sire be with thee, Michael Nero."

That was quite a speech, and I didn't need to hear any more from him. What he said was fine with me, since I didn't actually want to see him again for years, if ever, anyway. I took the folded bag he gave me and was now eager to get home and read the instructions on that scroll. Luckily, the required items didn't include any of that coyote piss, or any other kind of piss, for that matter. Then again, I really didn't want to know what type of stuff was in that ointment cocktail he gave me.

As I headed for the door that led out of the shop, I tapped Greydon on the shoulder, as he was still standing there like a statue staring at that gem. His eyes suddenly blinked a few times, as if he had just been awakened from a light sleep or heavy daydreaming session. He turned away from the glittering bauble by the front window that seemed to have stolen all his attention and followed me out the door. As we left, we both looked back at the front desk, where Rutger and I had sealed the deal. He was no longer there.

After we departed, Greydon asked about the bag in my hand.

"Did you get what you needed from him?"

"Yea, I did. Didn't you hear any of our conversation?"

"No, actually. That jewelry at the front was really cool, and I couldn't stop looking at it for some reason. How much did that whole package cost you?"

"Not much. I was able to afford it, luckily."

"Cool. So, then, can you still give me half of the finder's fee you owe me today?"

*Geez, this dude.*

\*\*\*

"Where are you going at this time of night?" my mother asked me as I headed out the door at 8 PM, with the satchel of items in hand. "And what do you have there?"

*Shit. It never fails.*

"I'm going over to Greydon's house. He loaned me this stuff from his chemistry kit and we're going to try to mix some... chemicals together. It's part of a lab project for Mr. Napolski's class."

"Why so late?"

"Because I wanted to eat dinner first, okay?"

"You usually go over there a lot earlier and eat over there if you stay late. His mom never seems to have a problem with having you stay for dinner if you're there."

"Well, he just got home. They were out somewhere."

"You know how dangerous it is walking down Niagara Street at this time of night! And he lives at the projects, and you always tell me how dangerous it is down there!"

My mother was right, of course. But I had to risk it, because I needed to be at the Waterfront by 11 PM, and she would have thrown an even bigger fit if I went out closer to that time. But I had to claim a trip to Greydon's house as a cover, and I was packing a switchblade I bought last week in case someone tried snatching the bag from me. But I needed to get there at the right time, or it would be a long while before the Moon and stars would be so properly lined up again to do the ritual correctly.

"I know about the dangers. I'll be careful, okay? But I have to go, I told him I would be there soon."

"You're carrying something, and someone might try to mug you for that bag! Let Frank drive you to Greydon's, okay?"

I couldn't have my stupid stepfather do that, because then he would find out I wasn't actually going to Greydon's, but all the way down to a secluded section of the Waterfront.

*Shit!*

"No, Mother! I have to go!"

"Have you even done your math homework yet?"

*She just had to start that shit, didn't she?*

13

"You know Mrs. Linsky called to tell me that you've already missed three assignments already! You're not going to pass math if you don't start doing that goddamned homework."

"I never pass math anyways! But I have to go, okay?"

Then that look I dreaded came on her face. "Get in here and do that homework. Right fucking now."

"I'll do it in the morning! I have to go now!"

"That's what you always say! Now get the fuck in here!"

Of course, she made a point to say it loud enough to get Frank's attention. That was never good. However, that just strengthened my resolve to get the ritual done and gain the power I believed would free me from all of this. *If* it worked. And if it didn't; well, then all I lost was the finder's fee I had to pay Greydon, and Rutger would lose all the shit he gave me with no 'Brotherhood of Fenris' commitment from me.

"What's the problem?" Frank said as he strode over, his nasty temper and muscular build quite intimidating to many men his own size, let alone a 13-year-old like me. "Are you talking back to your mother again?"

"He's going out with that shit Greydon gave him and won't do his homework tonight!" my mother spat. "I'm tired of this fucking kid!"

"All right, all right, I'll deal with this," Frank said, since he could see she was starting to go into one of her dramatic crying fits again. "Mike, get in here now! Don't make me come out there to get you!"

"You won't put your hands on me," I said.

"Don't give me a reason to, and I won't," he replied in a volatile tone.

The time was quickly passing, and I was not about to let him stop me. So, I began reaching into my pocket for the switchblade I had concealed there. *He better not make me use this! I won't let either of them hit me ever again.*

That potentially disastrous scenario was halted when my maternal grandfather, who lived downstairs from us (he owned the three-apartment house we lived in) stepped outside of his own back door to see what all the commotion was.

"What are you two maniacs screaming about?" he exclaimed. "The neighbors don't need to hear this and know how crazy you are! Or, to think I'm crazy for letting you live here!"

"It's that fucking grandson of yours again!" my mother all but screamed.

14

As my grandfather yelled at Frank and my mom, making them back away, I quickly ran out the backyard and towards Niagara Street.

"Mike, you little fuck, you!" my mother shrieked.

"Just let him go and stop screaming before you piss your father off even more," I could hear Frank's voice say as I exited the yard and disappeared down the block.

I was hoping and praying – to Fenris, mind you – that I wouldn't be too late. I now wanted that power promised me by Rutger more than ever.

\*\*\*

Thankfully, I had reached the designated area at the Marina without incident. I was highly relieved that I didn't have to use the switchblade to defend myself against *anyone* that particular night.

I stood in a small clearing at the park, which was deserted as per usual at this time of the night. I knew this since I often wandered there secretly after leaving Greydon's house to think and be alone, where I would dream of a moment like this coming my way. Now, it was almost upon me, and I was breathing so hard that I was besieged by heart palpitations.

I had stripped down to a pair of stretchy gym shorts and placed the pelt of genuine wolf hide around my waist, tightening it into a knot exactly as the parchment instructions described. I then took the small vial filled with rainwater that was allegedly scooped up from the pawprint of a wolf and poured it over my skull. Luckily, that water was warm, since it was damn cold outside that night, and I was beginning to shiver.

*Please let this work! And please let me get this finished at the right time, before one of those assholes comes looking for me; or someone finds me here doing this and calls the cops because they think I'm a crazy person, or whatever...*

I looked up in the sky to see the full moon nearing the apex of the stellar position it would be in when the final part of the ritual was to be conducted. I had just a few minutes left to finish prepping myself for the moment.

Next, I poured the wolf blood from another vial onto my hands. I smeared it all over my torso, arms, and legs as per the scroll's instructions. Then I shook up the oily tincture in the final bottle well and likewise smeared it all over me.

15

I had no idea exactly what was in that mixture, as the instructions simply said it was a bunch of herbs that were very "potent" and reactive to both the lunar energies and astronomical factors currently ruling the etheric forces that were currently flooding this side of the planet. The only herbs specifically listed in the scroll were wolfsbane, henbane, jimson weed, dragon's blood, cinque foil, and belladonna, some of which could be dangerous and/or psychoactive.

So, I was doing this at my own risk under the assumption that if conducted at the proper time while being suffused with the lunar energies and pouring intense emotional conviction into the ritual the end result would not be fatal. The scroll implied that there was more to the concoction than the above ingredients, and by not listing them I took it to imply that I might be hesitant to smear myself with the salve if I knew its entire composition.

With all of that done, I picked up a wooden wolf's-head charm that had certain sigils I did not recognize etched around its circumference, along with what looked like a string fetter around the neck area. The instructions said it was not meant to be worn as a necklace but to be held firmly in my "power hand" (being right-handed, that was the correct one for me), while bathing in the light of the full moon and intensely visualizing the growling image of Fenris's fierce canine features.

As the Moon reached its proper apex and the moment came, I did as instructed. I had to start rubbing the blood and herbal salve on me no more than ten minutes before that, since the potent mixture would begin taking effect after that point. Hence, it had to be done at *precisely* the right time, with no more than a scant few seconds of error.

Sure enough, several minutes after applying it I felt a strong, tingling, almost burning sensation all over my skin, accompanied by a light-headedness and strange spinning lights – almost akin to Fourth of July fireworks – begin rotating around the periphery of my vision. This threatened to overcome me, but as pissed off as I was before leaving the house, and with my mind filled with memories of the abuse I had taken through the years, my determination to follow through was strong.

I thus focused my will, envisaged the image of Fenris superimposed over the full moon while staring directly at it, and began chanting – not loudly, but quite firmly:

*"Fenris, Great Fenris, son of Loki, mutilator of Tyr, devourer of Odin at Ragnarok, hear my plea! Grant me thy power, thy ferocity, thy fleetness of foot, thy immense strength and stamina, thy oneness with the forces of nature. Suffuse me with the power of the luminous Eye of Odin, let me be thy avatar on Midgard and walk in thy form to aid all my mortal works. Make me forever one with the Wolf, in body and mind as needed, but let my own mind reign supreme. Give me thy power, thy majesty; grant it now and forevermore!"*

The burning sensation briefly became more intense, and I was suddenly filled with what felt like electrical energy crackling all through my fragile mortal form. It was as if the moonlight was now a regenerating beam, coursing through every cell, acting as a catalyst for strong chemical reactions in the mixture of blood and salve soaking into my skin, and instilling something extraordinary into me. My anger and fury at being so severely wronged suddenly escalated, and I wanted to tear my enemies to pieces and taste their flesh. I would accept nothing less than the power and form required to do all of that.

I opened my mouth to scream because of both the pain and the euphoria of power I was now feeling. As I heard my own deafening yell it soon segued from my regular voice into an animalistic snarl. I felt my body changing, pulling additional mass from realms unknown. I could literally feel my teeth and nasal area elongating, with my skull making cracking noises as the bones reconfigured.

I looked down at my hands to see a wondrous yet horrifying sight: my palms and fingers were enlarging while sprouting grayish fur from every single pore, and my fingernails were extending into razor sharp talons. The radical restructuring of my bones, musculature, teeth, and organs was clearly perceived as my body was drastically enhanced beyond human reason. This was accomplished by the essence of Fenris projected though the lunar energies and combining with the powerful mind-altering chemical agents now seeping into my skin, in accordance with my own focused emotions.

In less than a minute, the incredible metamorphosis was complete, and I looked to the glowing orb in the sky and called to it with a fearsome, reverberating howl. My vision was now extending into the infra-red spectrum as the heat images of everything became easily discernible. My muzzled snout picked up an amazing tapestry of scents barely noticeable or else entirely invisible to the human species, and my ears could detect sounds outside the mortal auditory range.

My sensory perceptions picked up the nighttime urban environment in far greater detail than ever before. I was aware of humans, animals, plants, and many other things well outside my line of sight simply by their scent and via a variety of sounds – everything from mice skittering across the dirt to the heartbeats of people to the point I could roughly distinguish their age, size, gender, and overall state of health from their individual tempos.

Strangest and most amazing of all, I was also somehow imbued with the *instincts* of the animal whose form I now mimicked, albeit a greatly enhanced, still partly anthropomorphic variation thereof. I knew how to use these new senses without having to train or learn in the manner that humans normally acquire their range of skills and knowledge. However, I also felt saturated with the ferocity and hunting inclinations of a wolf, all of which were amplified by my human rage.

I wanted to hunt something, someone; and my reigning human mind and the personality of Michael Nero struggled to get this new aspect of my psyche under control. As it turned out, at least at this early point in my transformation history, I was unable to suppress it, but could only *direct it* towards specific targets. Though I was at first standing comfortably on two legs much as I did as a human – if at a much greater height – I instinctively realized I would be just as comfortable with quadrupedal locomotion and would move much faster that way as well.

Hence, I slouched down to all fours and began running at a speed that surpassed any breed of dog in search of… something or some*one* to hunt down. Every step of the way, across the enormous range I could cover in a remarkably short time, my human mind struggled to maintain as much control as possible… as well as to fully process exactly what I had now become.

***

I couldn't help being impressed with myself for the speed I exhibited in reaching my planned destination. This would be a small arcade located on Niagara Street, a favorite haunt of mine, as well as that of other kids and the growing number of adult patrons who wanted to waste dozens of quarters on playing *Pac-Man, Donkey Kong,* and *Galaxian.* It was a place where I not only threw away so much spare change trying to master these new games that were taking the world by storm, but also a place where I inevitably ran afoul of numerous bullies. There were several other kids there of various age groups who gave me and others more than a simple hard time in the course of mooching quarters, ruining our games on purpose so they could play, and picking out "easy" targets to vent their personal frustrations on. One would be hard-pressed for a better place to find both good digital fun and a ready supply of victims than these arcades, especially at the smaller urban locations.

It was at this one, Dan's Place, that a few months earlier I was beaten up by several other teenagers. The thrashing I received would have been much longer and more severe if not for a Good Samaritan in the form of a bigger and older teen happening by and chasing them off. My mother and grandparents forbade me from going there again, and for a few months I complied – not because I was obedient, mind you, but simply because I was scared shitless of running into Ron Delaney and his cronies again.

This time, however, with the power of the lycanthrope in my grasp, I was heading towards that old haunt with the expressed hope of reacquainting with them. It was getting late, and the owner Dan usually locked up around 11 PM. But being the delinquents they were, Ron Delaney and his friends would often hang out around the place to smoke, talk, and heckle pedestrians walking by until close to midnight. It was one of those evenings after Dan locked up shop and departed that I got beat down right outside the arcade. And it was one of these nights where Ron and his friends-in-brutality were about to get some brutal comeuppance they could never expect.

As I ran through the nighttime streets, the natural instinct for stealth that came with the gift of Fenris enabled me to seek shortcuts through alleyways, crowded parking lots around supermarkets, and in and out of various backyards. There were relatively few people out and about at this time of night, and I moved fast enough on all fours that the few who caught a furtive glimpse of me racing by in the dark could easily mistake me for an unusually large dog. That was especially true with the canine panting and snarling sounds my no-longer-human larynx was making due to my animal side.

As I easily leapt over a six-foot-high wooden fence into an alley adjacent to a nearby backyard, I emerged in the section of Niagara Street just a few blocks from where Dan's Place was located. As I did so, I rushed by two walking pedestrians, likely a couple, and nearly knocked them over. I snarled in frustration but my human side kept my animalistic rage focused on my pre-designated targets, so I did not pounce on those two innocents.

Both the man and the women jumped back, thoroughly startled.

"What the fuck was that?" the man yelled.

"Some kind of dog or somethin'?" the woman hypothesized in response.

Before they could utter another word I was two blocks down and effectively outside their line of sight. I wondered what they thought they might have seen. In any event, I paid it no heed.

As I rushed across the street onto the block in the center of which was Dan's arcade, I surely enough caught sight of Ron Delaney and four of his partners, all of whom had participated in the beating I received months ago. Not only could I clearly discern them from that distance, their heat signatures keeping them overtly visible in the dark, but I could easily make out their voices. The youngest punk in the bunch, Marvin, bid them good night and began heading towards his home on Porter Avenue. I would track him after I dealt with Ron and the other three.

I dashed behind a nearby parked truck about twenty feet away and listened to their banter, sizing them up like the pieces of meat I now considered them. They were talking the usual shit about getting down the pants of girls, their recent high scores on *Pac-Man,* how they suspect that Dan is gay, and the latest ass-kicking they each delivered to some poor soul (with a 50/50 likelihood of being true). After a few minutes of that, I had heard enough. I also couldn't hold my animal side back any longer.

With a vicious snarl I rushed out from behind the truck and was on top of them a mere second before they saw me coming. I went for Ron, the alpha punk of the crew, first. I ripped into his denim jacket and thick sweater underneath with a quick slash of my front talons as I ran past him. He made a loud screech of agony and slunk down to his knees while grasping his bleeding stomach with both hands. The look on his face was priceless as his eyes bulged at the sight of his blood spilling out onto the street.

A second and a half later I tore into Brad, the tallest one, biting a chunk of flesh out of his left shoulder. He screamed in horror and pain while going down for the count on the hard concrete. I growled ferociously as I next slammed my furry canine head into Delgado, sending him flying across the sidewalk to land hard on his ass. My enhanced hearing could easily pick up the sound of his tailbone and pelvis cracking on impact.

The last one, Julio, who was nearly as tall as Brad, was startled as I stood up in a bipedal stance to tower over him by more than a foot and a half.

"Holy shit!" he shouted as he saw my muzzle filled with sharp teeth and my nearly luminous yellow eyes looking down at him.

I opened my maw to show the entirety of my teeth and growled to signal clear malicious intent at the trembling Julio.

"Oh, man, don't…" were the last words he uttered before transitioning into a scream as I lifted him off the ground and over my head as if he weighed mere ounces.

With a small effort, I hurled him clear through the front window of Dan's closed arcade. I could hear him yelling and writhing on the hardwood floor inside the place after the deed was done. I could also smell his spilled blood as a result of the broken glass cutting him all over.

I then turned back towards Ron, who was still on his knees holding his bleeding gut. I moved my large wolfen head less than an inch from his face and growled, wanting him to feel the full extent of my rage for what he had done to me. I couldn't speak in wolfen form at this point, so the tone of my roar had to replace the angry words I was thinking. He was obviously in a deep state of shock since he didn't react to this in any way. Instead, he just kept staring down with his wide, unblinking eyes at the square of sidewalk painted crimson with his blood.

Next door to Dan's Place was Mario's, a small family run pizzeria that was still open. The owner and manager, Mario Gambino, was present and heard the ruckus going on next door to him. He ran outside brandishing a metal pipe he kept on hand as a weapon only to see a wolf-like monstrosity (that was me) standing over the injured and bleeding bodies of three teenagers, and the shards of Dan's front window scattered onto the sidewalk (courtesy of Julio being hurled through it by yours truly).

"Hey!" Mario yelled while raising the pipe. "Get away from those boys!"

21

Big mistake on his part. With my rage now focused on him, I snarled at the brave man while rising to a bipedal stance again.

"Jesus and Mary!" the burly Italian guy shouted at the impossible sight before him.

The animal side of me wanted to leap on this foolish prick and make him pay for challenging me. My human side did its best to stop it. *Mike, hold up! That's Mario. He was always nice to you when you ate at his pizzeria. I… won't do it. I'm gonna go hunt Marvin instead. I got his scent.*

The wolf I now was growled angrily at Mario. He shuddered and moved back a step, but stood firm with his pipe still raised, ready to fight for both his life and that of the punks he knew and disliked. Something about that struck me, just as his past kindness to me did. After a few tense moments my human side won out, and I turned and dashed away on all fours. Within seconds I had disappeared from Mario's field of vision.

"Dear Jesus…" the thickly mustached cook whispered to himself before running back into his pizzeria to call both an ambulance and the police.

\*\*\*

It turned out I had lost Marvin's trail, or he had gone indoors before I could find him. So, I opted for tearing apart a small stray dog I came across that was raiding someone's garbage. I had never killed anything bigger than an insect before that, and I was amazed at the sheer ecstatic zeal I displayed while digging into the mutt's entrails. This act of mini-carnage did, however, satisfy my lust for the hunt that night. It was just past 1 AM when I rushed into my own backyard by leaping over several of my neighbors' the backyard fences. Evidently, my wolf-like stealth and speed paid off, as no one saw me coming back to "home base." Once I was in the yard, I faced the next step in learning to navigate what I had now become: turning back to human form.

With the savage need for the hunt fulfilled, and the animal side now appeased, I found that my human mind was almost completely ascendant. Provided, that is, nothing else appeared to threaten me or piss me off. The coast seemed clear in the early morning darkness of my backyard, however. As the scroll instructed, all I had to do was either wait for sunrise or assert my human side and focus intently on the image of the full moon waning until it went completely dark (i.e., phased into a new moon).

I did that, and within moments I felt the sheer power I had amassed draining from me. That is the closest I can describe this downbeat sensation. I could feel the other-dimensionally accrued mass leaving my body and my anatomy reconfiguring into standard human. It was uncomfortable but only slightly painful – nothing I couldn't handle. Within several moments I felt much less powerful and the chill of the Buffalo October night on my now hairless skin made me realize I was entirely human and pathetically mortal again. I felt both relieved and vulnerable at the same time. The steam I let off, the vengeance I gained while hunting, was something I knew I would need to do again soon. The animal part of my persona was subordinate to the human side, but it still called to me with a stern demand to be regularly freed from its human cage.

I felt over my hips and was doubly relieved to notice the stretchy gym shorts I put on before transforming were intact. The dark bluish gray of the cloth was likely all but invisible to onlookers in my werewolf form, especially when I was moving quickly. I took care to tear the labels off so there wouldn't be a brand symbol on it that might ever be seen or photographed as a mark of identification to something I was known to wear. During my last trek to the mall I made a point to buy several pairs of these cheap but durable shorts with zipper pockets so I could secure house keys, a bit of money, a switchblade, and other small items inside the pants.

As I took out my keys and headed towards the entrance to my mom's apartment from the backyard, I suddenly halted when the back door to my grandparents' residence opened. Out came my grandfather, who decided this night of all nights to do one of his late evening rakings of the front lawn before the full winter weather hit. *Son. Of. A. Bitch.*

I dashed around the corner of the huge tool shed attached to the back of the house just before he saw me. My keys jingled in my hands for a second, and he turned briefly to see what the sound was. *Shit, is he gonna come back here and look? Do I have to make a dash for the fence leading to the next yard? Climbing it in human form is gonna be a bitch. And I'm fuckin' freezing here!*

23

Thankfully, the powerfully built guy a few years short of his 50s decided not to inspect the sound and instead carry on with his evening lawn work. He took the rake he kept against the back section of the house and carried it out front. I peered as carefully as I could behind the corner of the house, freezing my ass off the entire time, while impatiently waiting for him to leave the yard.

Then I unlocked the back door leading to the stairway into my mom's apartment as quietly as I could, shut and relocked the door, and carefully moved up the stairs. If my mother or Frank caught me walking in at this time of the night in nothing but these shorts, without even shoes or socks on, I would be in the dank pits of shit hell.

Obviously, my mother, at least, would be awake for as long as I was out. I heard her television on in her room and could see the light of the tube flickering out the mostly open door as I stepped into the house. I tiptoed into my room and threw on a spare set of clothing that resembled what I had on when I left. This included a pair of sneakers other than the cheap $5.00 pairs I picked up at the Main Center Mall for my activities this night, knowing I would lose them. Then I tiptoed back to the entrance of the back door, opened it again, then closed it louder, so my mother would hear and think I was just walking in.

"Do you know how late it is?" my mother hollered as she came storming out of her room at the sound.

"I know how to read a clock," I rejoined.

"It's a school night! Do you know how hard it's going to be to get you up in the morning?"

"So, let's save this argument 'til I wake up, like we usually do."

"You little fuck!" she yelled as I closed my door. "I'm telling Frank!"

On hearing that, it seemed as if my animal side suddenly re-asserted itself. I actually gritted my teeth and snarled slightly despite being in human form. I slipped my fingers into my pocket so I was in contact with the switchblade I had kept secure there during my transformation. I waited a few minutes to see if Frank would get up and confront me.

He didn't.

Lucky him.

\*\*\*

I managed to get almost six hours of sleep, and that sufficed. I turned on the bulky TV set in my room to watch the morning news I was looking forward to hearing. My heart was racing in anticipation of what the announcer would say on Channel 7's Eyewitness News AM. I grinned with satisfaction when the top story of the morning was exactly what I anticipated.

"Topping this morning's news," said announcer Kathleen Evans, "a grisly attack on four teenaged boys occurred on Niagara Street late in the evening, right in front of the Dan's Place arcade and next door to Mario's Pizza. The attack resulted in serious wounds for all four victims, with one apparently thrown through the front window of Dan's Place, which occurred after closing time when the proprietor, Dan Collins, had left for the evening.

"The only witness to the attack was Mario Gambino, the owner of the pizzeria next door. He gave his description to the Eyewitness News reporters on the scene, and what he described was a chilling sight."

The screen shifted to footage of Mario's familiar face as he struggled to control his excitement and fear over what he had seen to describe it to the reporter's mic being held in front of his face.

"I know what I saw, and I wouldn't lie to the people of this city. It looked like a wolf, a really large wolf. It was huge and... muscular. It looked like it was covered in grayish fur. Really big and nasty-looking. It growled at me like it wanted to attack me next. And it... stood up on two legs, like a man. Just like a man! And its back legs were like a dog's, but it looked like it had hands like a person instead of front paws. Really big hands, with claws! I thought it was going to kill me!"

"Are you sure it wasn't just a big dog, Mr. Gambino?" the reporter asked him. "Maybe foaming at the mouth, like it had rabies?"

"No, I tell you!" Mario replied firmly. "It wasn't foaming, and it stood up like a man! On two legs! It tossed one of the boys through Dan's front window! What kind of dog throws people through a window?"

"Did you actually see the animal throw the boy, Mr. Gambino?" the reporter queried.

"Well, no! But that's obviously what it did!"

"Are you sure the boy didn't simply leap through the window in an attempt to get away from the vicious dog attack?"

"No! I mean, I don't think so. I know that thing threw him! It stood up like a man, it was huge and it had hands! I thought it was gonna kill me!"

"Thank you for your report, Mr. Gambino."

"The people of this city need to be warned! There's some kind of monster on the loose!"

The screen then cut back to blonde-haired Kathleen Evans. "We sternly believe this was an attack by a feral dog, as a few such attacks by an alleged pack of stray dogs were reported over the last month."

*Really? Hmmm, that's interesting.*

"Though we believe this was another feral dog attack, which Mr. Gambino mistook for something worse while confronting the animal in the midst of the darkness and his panic, there was a reported sighting of an alleged 'wolf monster' by a couple who said the beast emerged from an alley and ran past them snarling at, I quote, 'a whacked out speed.' It was likely another sighting of a feral dog and shines interesting light on what people may think they see if startled by the sudden appearance of a large canine while walking about in the dark."

I grinned. *That would be the couple I almost knocked over when I rushed out of the alley. Ha ha. How cool was that? And should I have killed Ron and his fellow assholes? I wanted to. But... I think what I did do was enough. As long as I never see them around again. Next, I'm gonna hunt down Marvin, the last of Ron's crew. Then, I'll find Dean O'Sullivan and sink my claws into him. And if those assholes at school keep up their shit with me...*

As I was getting ready for school, my mother naturally got on my case, as she didn't leave for work until later. Thankfully, Frank had left for his job before I got up.

"Did you hear about what happened last night at that arcade where you used to hang out?" she asked me.

"Yea, I heard it on the news this morning. Some punks got torn up."

"It could have been you! That was the same route you take to walk to Greydon's house!"

"It was quiet on Niagara Street when I went to his house. And you know I don't hang at that arcade anymore. Not since I got beat up there."

"Did you hear about those 'wolf man' sightings?"

"Yea, I heard about them. I gotta go to school now. I'll miss the bus if I don't leave right now."

"You go to school. But Frank is going to have a word with you when you get home."

I turned to the mother I never got along with and gritted my teeth at her. "I'd keep him away from me if I were you."

"I'm going to tell him you said that!"

"Keep him away from me. I mean it."

After saying that, I ignored my mother's swearing tirade and left for school.

\*\*\*

It's difficult to describe how I felt at school the day after the first transformation. Though I looked to them like I always had – a skinny, not overly tall white kid with dark hair – I was no longer a pathetic loser scrambling at the bottom of the social totem pole. I was now something far more than they were. I had to find a way to let them know it without revealing myself to the higher up's at the school, or the law. I needed to let them know I was now the alpha in a way they would understand but which could not be proven by the adults with the real authority. I could take out a whole group of those adults too, but I wasn't keen on going up against guns, even if the bullets weren't silver. And if any of them ever came to accept the reality of a werewolf in their midst, I would eventually have to deal with authorities armed with silver weaponry, which the scroll made clear would be lethal to a werewolf.

As I walked down the corridor to my locker, I spotted Maddy Mainfield at hers. Feeling bolder now that I saw myself as an alpha, I felt I should act the part. So, I approached her with the intention to let my interest be officially known and even ask her out. I felt that might actually take more guts than going through with the ritual the other night considering my past success with girls… as in, the lack thereof.

And Maddy was truly stunning to behold. She was about an inch and a half taller than me, with the most amazing shoulder length reddish-auburn hair, a perfect body, bright blue eyes, and the cutest freckled face to compliment her pale skin.

"Hey, Maddy," I said to her with a smile. "How are you doing?"

27

"Mike?" she replied, as if surprised I had approached her. "Hi."

"I'm glad I ran into you before classes. I was wondering if you'd like to, um, do something together one of these days."

"Huh?"

I went red. "Oh, I meant, like, have lunch together or get a pizza together, or something like that. My treat!"

She glared at me with those amazing blue eyes, not quite sure she could actually be hearing what she was indeed actually hearing.

"Um, Mike... I have a boyfriend."

"Really? Word has it that you broke up with that Mark guy a few months ago. I heard you mention that to Sally last week in language arts class."

"Okay. But I heard this other guy is going to ask me out, and I really want to go out with him, so I can't see anyone else until I hear from him."

"Well, what if weeks go by and he never asks you?"

"I don't know, alright?"

The increasingly unpleasant conversation was interrupted when I was suddenly pushed into the metal locker door next to Maddy's. I hit with enough force that I fell to the floor, a familiar location for me to end up when Al Jenning was around. Of course, his main sidekick-in-crime David Conroy was right beside him.

"Leave Maddy alone!" Al angrily demanded. "I'm sick of you bothering her all the time."

"Kick his ass, Al!" David exclaimed, hoping to egg his friend on.

Suddenly, I felt a rage welling up inside me that that quickly overshadowed the fear of the bigger peer. The animal that now co-habited my psyche had been "poked." I gritted my teeth while looking up at Al and made a snarling sound.

"Ha ha! Check it out!" David said. "The fag thinks he's a wolf or something!"

"Yeah," Al concurred, "he must have heard about the West Side Wolf Man from the news. Now he thinks he's all 'bad' like the wolf man!"

Then, without warning, without any further thought on my part, I jumped to my feet and socked Al right in his acne-scarred face. I managed to hit with startling force due to the adrenalin-driven ferociousness the animal side was sending through my human form. The taller boy was sent back against the lockers on the other side of the corridor. He slumped to the floor, now learning what it was like to be laying there, after slamming into one of the metal doors. He rubbed his hand over his nose and was again startled when he found blood pouring from both nostrils.

"Whoa!" David shouted.

"Al…" Maddy murmured.

The tough athletic teen pushed himself back to his feet and looked me in the eyes. "You're fucking dead."

"Yea?" I replied defiantly, my fists clenched and my teeth gnashed. "Maybe I'll kill *you* instead!"

Al and I charged each other and found ourselves grappling against the locker doors. Al punched me in the chest, but I weathered the pain, grabbed his arm, and bit into his hand. He shouted in pain as my human teeth broke the skin and made him bleed for the second time in a minute.

It was then that Mr. Simmons the social studies teacher and Mr. Woodman the hall monitor pulled us apart. They had to put both of us up against the lockers several feet apart to settle us down.

"Go to your classes!" Mr. Simmons shouted at the gathering crowd of students in the hallway.

He then turned to Al. "You're going to the nurse's office, Al."

"I don't need to go!" he shouted.

"Yes, you do," Simmons insisted. "You're bleeding out the nose and from your hand where he bit you. Now, let's go! Mr. Woodman, please deal with that one."

"C'mon, young man," Woodman said as he pulled me down the corridor by the shoulder. "You're going to the office, and you can look forward to a suspension."

Maddy stood outside her first period classroom door watching as Al and I were dragged away in opposite directions. The look of fear on her face was palpable.

"I'll call you, Al," she said to the tall boy as Simmons escorted him to the nurse's office.

Now I was even more pissed at Al.

*We'll see which of the two of us ends up "dead," you asshole.*

\*\*\*

No sooner did I get out of the car after my fuming mother drove me home than I saw Marvin talking to my cousin Tish. She was a year younger than me, and she and her mom lived in the third apartment within the house my grandfather owned. As we entered our adolescent years we began growing further apart, particularly due to the company she kept. Among them was Marvin, who she was friends with despite knowing he had bullied me in the past and participated in the group ass-kicking I received months earlier. He attended her middle school (a different one from Woodlawn), and this wasn't the first time I saw him around the house.

*But it will be the last,* I thought to myself.

"I'm sorry about what happened to your cousin and his friends," I heard Tish say to Marvin, in reference to what I did to Julio and his cronies in werewolf form the previous night.

"They'll be good," he said. "And we'll find and kill what did that to them."

*Yea, right! We'll see, asshole.*

As Marvin began leaving, I stopped in front of Tish.

"Get in this fucking house!" my mother screamed at me.

I ignored her and told Tish, "I don't want that Marvin around this house anymore."

"He's my friend!" she replied curtly.

"He's one of those assholes who beat me up at the arcade months ago!" I shouted back. "And you're still hanging out with him after he did that to family?"

"Hey, he didn't do it to me," she said.

"I don't want him around here anymore!" I insisted louder than before.

"I said, get in this house!" my mother shouted again.

My anger began welling up again, and without thinking I shot after Marvin before he was more than halfway down the block.

"Hey, Marvin!" I yelled.

"What do you want?" he asked after turning around.

"What I want is for you to stay away from my house! After what you did to me, you have a lot of balls to come around here!"

"I'm Tish's friend, and she don't' seem to mind," he replied. "So, fuck off, man."

"Well, *I mind,*" I said as my rage began taking over again. "Don't let me see you around my neighborhood again."

"What are you gonna do about it, mother fucker?" he said after stepping up to me.

Suddenly my mother grabbed me and pulled me back before I could follow through with my intention of biting the tip of his nose off.

"You get out of here!" my mother screamed at Marvin. "Get out!"

Marvin walked away in a huff while my mother dragged me towards the house.

"Aunt Ann," Tish said, "Marvin's my friend. Mike can't tell me who I can bring around here, can he? My mother said I can bring anyone I want around."

"Get in there!" my mother shouted at me, ignoring Tish and pointing to the backyard leading to the entrance into our house.

While she was getting ready to bitch me out for the suspension I earned at school, all I was thinking about was the hunt that evening. Marvin would be the target, as I now had his scent.

*\*\*\**

That night I ducked into an alley down the street from my house, one heavily shrouded with overgrown foliage. After checking to make sure no bum had made it their home for the night, I stripped down to my gym shorts and took to summoning the wolf for the second time. The scroll told me it would be easier from the second occasion onward, as I only had to do the full ritual to alter my body chemistry while bonding with the animal spirit once.

I focused and concentrated on an image of the full moon, mentally called upon the power of Fenris, and drew down the lunar energies washing over the planet (which was actually reflected sunlight whose photonic composition was altered by deflection off the Moon's mineral surface, in case anyone cared to know that.) The powerful tingling and burning sensation washed over me much as it did the night before, and within just under a minute the amount of lunar energy on the first night of the full moon was sufficient to cause the transformation without undue difficulty.

31

Within moments, my body was transfigured as the lunar radiations and the psychic energies of Fenris suffused my every cell. I growled fiercely as the animal side that now shared my psyche rose from near-dormancy and spurred me into the hunt.

I avoided exiting the alley from the front, but instead by leaping over a few backyard fences that allowed me to reach the streets a good distance away from my own neighborhood. I sniffed the air and ground as I did so while moving in the direction of Porter Avenue, hoping to catch Marvin's scent. Finally, I caught it. It was obvious he had walked up Niagara towards where several of his friends lived on Porter, so I took up the trail.

Suddenly, I caught a whiff of a very distinctive odor... that of human blood. A lot of it. It was also mixed with a specific human scent. So, I followed it only to find that it led into an alley near Busti Avenue. It was there I came upon the remains of Marvin.

I could only tell it was him by his scent because his body was torn to pieces. His stomach was ripped open, clear through his jacket, and his bowels were sprawled over his chest. The boy's throat was ripped open and all four of his limbs were partially eaten, gnawed right down to the bone. His blood was spattered everywhere on the filthy concrete around him.

Startled, I wondered what could have done this. However, rather than getting sick at the sight and smell, as I likely would have had I been in human form, in my wolfen form I instead began salivating.

*Had I done this to Marvin after first going out tonight in wolfen form, and not remembered, because the animal side took over completely? But I wouldn't have gone that far! I would have stopped myself! I succeeded in stopping myself with his cousin and their three friends the other night. I didn't do this... because I wouldn't have!*

Suddenly, my human side began taking over as the animal aspect of my psyche was beaten back by the confusion – and possibly, remorse – that was now flowing through my mind like a river loosed from a broken dam.

If I didn't do this to Marvin in wolfen form, then what did? The answer soon came my way when I turned at the sound of panting behind me. What I saw was a group of three feral dogs. The trio seemed to consist of a German shepherd, a rottweiler, and a slightly smaller dog of a breed I couldn't identify. My human mind didn't seem to operate at full cognitive capacity in my lupine form, but close enough unless I really lost it.

This trio of canines didn't react in fear to the sight of a werewolf, which dogs would normally do, automatically recognizing a lycanthrope as the equivalent of an alpha canine in their presence. Instead, they growled fiercely at me. I could see their slavering jaws were coated with Marvin's blood, and their coats stank of his scent. *They* had done this to him, not my wolfen alter-ego.

Before I could react further the German shepherd and smaller dog charged at me. They barreled into my bulky form, their combined speed and force taking me by surprised and toppling me over. The first one bit into my furry arm, while the second clamped its jaws onto my wolf-like leg. The rottweiler barked and growled, looking around for an entrance into the melee. The pain rekindled my rage, and I let my animal side take over completely. Which was wise.

I used my supernaturally strong arm to pull the clamped German shepherd towards my lupine muzzle. I then bit into the animal's throat and tore it out with a single heave of my wolfen head. The dog let out a brief yelp and fell onto the ground dead.

The other dog kept pulling at the flesh of my leg, so I slumped forward and pummeled its head with my large, human-shaped hand. The blows rivaled that of a gorilla in strength, and just a few of them crushed the animal's skull, sending blood and brain matter spewing out its ears while its eyes popped out of their sockets.

Before I could catch a breath, however, the rottweiler tore into me with savage fury. The impressive jaw strength I had always heard that this breed possessed was amply demonstrated as it locked onto my right arm… the one I was barely fast enough to cover my throat with, which was the dog's actual target.

Though a werewolf is powerful enough to give a grizzly bear pause, I was nevertheless a juvenile specimen, not yet up to my full strength. I needed to be careful when I was up against heavy opposition. And three rogue dogs seemed to fit that bill, especially when one of them was a rottweiler.

I felt the flesh surrounding my arm get torn off as the powerful black dog continued its attack, but thankfully my supernaturally strong bones held. I didn't know for how long they would, however, so I let my rage grow to full intensity. I released a bellowing howl of fury as I punched at the rottweiler's head several times.

It took several blows, but finally the mighty canine was forced to release the vice-like grip of its jaws after sustaining a serious concussion. The dog was still not out, however. Something spurred it on, forcing it not to retreat, and keeping its rage focused on tearing me apart. It was something as seemingly unnatural to the world as a werewolf.

Undaunted as a result of this, the dog renewed its bloody assault. I knew better than to let it sink its jaws into my flesh again, especially not my throat. So, I met its charge on four legs, and my longer muzzle closed tightly about the dog's neck before it could get a grip on mine.

I then stood on two legs and lifted the dog into the air. I slashed at its exposed belly with my talons, slicing open its abdomen and watching its bowels spill out onto the ground – doing to it precisely what it had done to Marvin earlier. I then shook its neck in my jaws, ripping open its throat and tasting its blood, which excited the hunter aspect of my persona. I then let its lifeless, mutilated body drop to the ground like a discarded laundry sack.

The nasty wounds inflicted on my arm and leg were already beginning to heal with supernatural rapidity, but they still hurt like hell. I nevertheless howled my victory to the starry sky. After the dominance of the wolf psyche subsided and my human persona took near-full control, I was forced to wonder what set these dogs off and caused them to form a pack that not only hunted and preyed on humans, but would unhesitatingly stand up to a werewolf.

Again, I would receive my answer within seconds. And it was one that chilled even my wolfen alter-ego down to the very marrow of my bones.

I heard another dog growling at the alley's entrance, this one sounding deeper and even more fierce than the previous three combined. I focused my keen night vision to the front of the path, which enabled me to see the heat outline of the mystery canine. It was a very big one, lean but powerfully built. Its eyeshine reflected off the glare of the nearby streetlights and penetrated the front of the alley like twin lasers. I could see the outline of its teeth as it snarled what was obviously a warning, as if to make it clear that it was not me who was the alpha predator of the Queen City.

My unexpected canine opponent, obviously the leader of the pack, moved its head further into the alley to do a better job of sizing up the lycanthropic opposition before it. That was when I got a better look at the animal, though not a complete one. What I did see, however, suggested a force to be reckoned with.

Its head was narrow, ugly, and terrifying. It had a coat of very short reddish fur, pale hazel eyes, and a long muzzle filled with sharp teeth that resembled ivory daggers. Its height, despite being on four legs, was close to five feet, if not exceeding that. It looked like a Vizsla in breed, but much nastier, if that made sense. It was then that I realized exactly what I was looking at; or, more specifically, *who.*

My now ascendant human mind recalled the legend of a killer canine that haunted the urban locale of Buffalo's West Side that I grew up in. It was one that my childhood friend Chuck Heino described to me back in the day, and which he and I actually saw twice. We were lucky we weren't killed during that second encounter, but that is a story unto itself. What I was seeing now, however, was an adversary of the canine variety that even a werewolf would fear to oppose, as it seemed even larger and fiercer than what I recalled seeing years before.

*The Jack Dog,* I said to myself. *I thought he was put down years ago after he escaped from those people who bred him. But... this can only be him. And after my rumble with those other three dogs, I'm in no shape to take on the Jack Dog himself. I am totally in a world of shit.*

Just then, the sound of approaching police sirens filled the night air. Their piercing echo was particularly rough on the ears of those with the keen level of hearing shared by me and the adversary I now faced. The Jack Dog released one more warning growl, this one deeper and more ferocious than before, and retreated from the alley and down the street at a speed that even I may not be able to match in lupine form.

I followed suit and ran to the back of the alley. There I leapt over a tall metal fence and disappeared down the street to find a place to hide while my wounds healed. I wanted them to heal as much as possible before rushing home and reverting to human form. I also had to gather my thoughts about what I had just went up against. I had a mission of revenge against people who had hurt me in the past, but the presence of the Jack Dog and the pack of feral dogs he controlled presented a threat that not even the powerful werewolf I had become was safe from.

\*\*\*

Interestingly, when Rutger "sold" me that package of items, he tossed in a few old tomes on the occult (which must have been the "bonus" he mentioned). The instructions on the scroll noted that I should study this literature and become as adept at mysticism as I possibly could. This was due to the fact that I was a shamanistic lycanthrope, not the cursed variety who became what they were involuntarily and whose plight became popularized by Hollywood during the course of the 20th century. Shamanistic werewolves, however, took on the mantle of the *loup garou* entirely of their own volition, and we thus enjoyed much better control and more versatile use of our animalistic alter-ego than our cursed brethren typically did. Our legends primarily unfolded not in Hollywood depictions of both real and false tales, but in the pages of folklore. This is why a book on Slavic shape-shifter legends, both of werewolves and were-bears (the berserkers), was also included by Rutger in the life-changing satchel he gave me. I was also encouraged to conduct further research and study of magick and folklore beyond the volumes he provided.

However, one particular book that Rutger included was a volume detailing the folklore, legends, and strange facts of Western New York, where I was born and raised. Within those pages I quickly learned that this area was a hotbed of strange occurrences, which means Buffalo and its surrounding environs is a "window area" for Fortean phenomena. In other words, paranormal, supernatural, and just plain strange events tend to occur here with regularity; and odd entities and individuals tend to be either drawn to the area from outside source or actually born within its confines – everything from monsters, to UFO/alien activity, mystics, serial killers, ghost manifestations, dimensional portals unexpectedly opening to God-knows-where… a veritable grab bag of high strangeness that included, um, me, I suppose.

It was explained in my extensive research that the term "Fortean," taken from the surname of the late Charles Fort, an author who studied and catalogued such phenomena in the earlier part of the 20th century, was

36

applied to such paranormal or otherwise strange manifestations. He wrote three books on the topic that I scoured the local libraries for to no avail, so I had to have each of them ordered from outside the state.

The local vicinity of my neighborhood and the surrounding 'hoods were a key example of the Queen City strangeness. The Holy Apostate School I attended for three years, and which was a source of so much trauma to me related to bullying, was the location of an insane asylum in the late 19th century and into the early part of this one. Strange deaths had occurred there, including both homicides and suicides, and this is why the grounds and the surrounding area are said to be haunted by ghostly apparitions – some of which I had actually seen during my time as a student there, and even before that at a nearby orphanage on Porter Avenue.

As a voracious reader with the strong intention to study writing, both scholarly and otherwise, I ate this material up fast. As a shamanistic lycanthrope, I had started on the road to becoming a mystic, and that additional tool kit of knowledge would add to the power of the wolf, making the use of my transformations that much more versatile over time, as well as giving me a whole other set of capabilities. That is, if I would survive long enough into the future to reach that point, which I was now determined to do. It was a welcome alternative to the self-pity and suicidal thoughts that previously permeated my daydreams.

Which brought me to one particular legend regarding local Queen City strangeness that I needed to focus on: The Jack Dog. The legend of this canine monstrosity had long been the terror of the very neighborhood I lived in, and it was first brought to my attention by my childhood friend and frequent partner-in-mischief Chuck Heino. I knew I had to seek him out to revisit the subject, which was easy to do since he still lived in the same 'hood.

When I saw him outside the following day, I quickly made my presence known to Chuck in my own inimitable fashion. I unexpectedly tackled him from behind and put him in a tight pincer hold. He was bigger and stronger than me, and he could take it, so why not?

"Gotcha!" I said as I put him in the hold. "Let's see you break this one! Hah!"

"Can you let me go?" Chuck asked. "Because, well, you're hugging me sorta, and I don't want anyone to see this and think that I'm, ya know…"

"Ha ha ha!"

Since I had business to discuss, after I got my laugh I released him as requested to begin discussing it. He had a question for me first, though.

"Did you hear about the wolf man sightings?"

"Yea, I did. What I wanted to talk to you about, though, is the Jack Dog. Rumor has it he's back again. And that he's formed a pack out of stray and abandoned dogs that he's turned into killers."

"I wouldn't be surprised. You remember when we saw him years ago. He was supposed to have been put down by the police after a helluva battle[1], but his owners may have bred another one."

"Yea, about those people you told me were responsible for breeding the Jack Dog and making it 'go crazy.' Who were they? Why the hell would they breed a dog like that in the first place?"

"I dunno who they were. I hardly ever saw them, remember? I heard they were supposed to be professional dog breeders gone crazy, or just evil, or really weird or something. I think maybe they were witches, like those two hag sisters that used to live down the street here until… well, you know[2].

"But anyways, even though I don't have the full story, I know they bred that thing in their house on purpose, and made sure it was bigger, stronger, and crazier than most any other dog that ever lived. They had it trained to kill, but it was so crazy that after a while they lost control and it started getting out of the house when they didn't want it to. That's when all the bad shit started happening 'till the cops killed it. Not before it killed some of them first, though."

"So, you think they could have bred another one?"

"Oh, yeah. Maybe it has something to do with those wolf man sightings."

"Well, not directly."

"How could you know that for sure?"

---

[1] That is quite a tale indeed, but for another time and book. Hint: Look for the upcoming horror anthology series *Mansion of the Macabre* from Wild Hunt Press!

[2] Yet another interesting tale for another time.

I bit my lip. "Maybe the appearance of the West Side Wolf Man acted as, yanno, a catalyst for its reappearance. Remember that strange events in certain 'window areas' tend to result in other strange events happening that do not even appear to come from the same source. But since reports of dog pack attacks in the city go back a few months before the wolf man sightings, the catalyst could maybe have been the other way around."

"Not that stuff again. You really read too much."

"It's a 'fault' I don't mind having."

"It's a really fucking annoying fault," came a voice from behind us. It was none other than our sometimes friend, sometimes nemesis Marcus Gekko.

Marcus was a foul-mouthed kid my age who used to attend Holy Apostate School with me. He always tended to pop up unexpectedly and hear things that were better kept away from his ears.

"And speaking of strange," Marcus continued, "did you notice the kids that wolf man ripped into just happened to be the same ones that beat the shit out of you at the arcade a few months ago?"

"That is a strange coincidence, yea," I replied a bit nervously.

"It didn't kill them, but it really fucked them up," Marcus added. "But it totally slaughtered Marvin, who was the last one of them, the night after."

"It was the Jack Pack that did that!" I firmly insisted.

"What the fuck is the 'Jack Pack'?" the dark-haired kid queried.

"I think it's what he's calling the pack of dogs that the Jack Dog might be controlling," Chuck correctly guessed.

"That's a corny ass name," Marcus said. "Sounds like something a faggot would come up with. And besides, the Jack Dog was killed years ago."

"We think maybe they bred another one," Chuck said.

"Those crazy bastards that lived around the corner from here?" Marcus stated. "Why didn't they get arrested or shot by the cops when that shit went down?"

"Word has it there was no proof they intended the Jack Dog to turn out the way it did," I mentioned. "Or, some legal loophole of some sort I didn't really understand."

"Which was bullshit," Chuck insisted. "They knew what they were doing. Or they thought they did, until it all went to hell for them too."

39

"Wait," Marcus said, getting back to a previous topic with me. "How would you know if it was the Jack Dog's gang that tore up Marvin instead of the wolf man? And how would you know it was the wolf man that ripped into the other ones the night before and not this new Jack Dog?"

"Because according to the reports," I reminded him, "the wolf man… doesn't kill. He hurts, but he doesn't kill. He… hasn't gone that far. But the Jack Pack is known to kill, or at least try to."

"Then how do you know if it didn't *try* to kill Julio and his crew until Mario chased it away?" Marcus just refused to drop that uncomfortable line of interrogation.

"Because the Jack Dog wouldn't have thrown someone through a window!" I exclaimed.

"And how do you know that part of the story isn't a crock of shit?" Marcus asked. "That reporter said Julio might've jumped through the window while trying to get away."

"That would have been a totally crazy thing to do!" I insisted.

"Well, Julio was a crazy mother fucker," Marcus noted. "And he was scared shitless at the time. Or, maybe Mario broke the window when he threw a brick at the thing, but didn't mention that so Dan wouldn't sue his ass for the damage."

"Mario didn't throw a brick at the wolf man!" I said with more frustration. "He threatened it with that lead pipe he keeps in his pizzeria to chase the punks away."

"Yeah? And how could you possibly know that?" Marcus inquired with a strong look of suspicion. "He didn't mention the pipe in the report. I know, 'cause I watched it."

"Well, it's just logical to assume that," I replied, "because he always kept that pipe around for self-defense."

"Is it?" Marcus remarked as he looked at me with even greater suspicion.

*This is not good. I mean, I want everyone to know I have power eventually, but I want it to be done on my own terms. And what is he gonna think after he hears that the wolf man gets Dean O'Sullivan?*

"I think if the Jack Dog is back, this could all be the work of him and his pack," Chuck opined. "The wolf man sightings could just be of the Jack Dog. He's huge like a wolf! Maybe bigger."

*Thank you, man!*

40

"As I remember, the Jack Dog doesn't look anything like a fuckin' wolf," Marcus pointed out.

"But still," Chuck added, "this all happened in the dark and he attacks really fast. And like you said, the witnesses were all scared shitless at the time."

*Thanks for adding reasonable doubt into this, Chuck!*

"Mario said it looked like a wolf, and stood on two legs like a man," Marcus explained. "The Jack Dog never stands on two feet like that. And those others that saw it said it was really shaggy and grayish. The Jack Dog is not shaggy, it isn't grayish, and it don't look like no fucking wolf. It's one of those big ass, short-haired, red-headed dogs."

"It moves fast, though, and like I said, it was dark," Chuck mentioned.

"Chuck has a really good point!" I quickly said. "And anyways, I have to go now because I have things to do. I'll catch up with you fine gents later."

"See ya," Chuck replied.

"And stop talking like a faggot!" Marcus shouted at me. "That's why they always picked on you!"

"Oh, will you stop with that shit!" I said. "I swear, it's gotten so that if you so much as sneeze a certain way, people accuse you of being 'gay.' I don't even know what a 'faggot' is supposed to be anymore! Later, man!"

I still couldn't help noting the deep suspicious look Marcus gave me as I walked away. Did he think I was something more than just a "faggot?" I realized I needed to keep an eye on him, just as I knew he would be keeping one on me.

\*\*\*

The following night would be a dramatic one. I was determined to sink my claws into Dean O'Sullivan, no matter the dangers of Marcus's suspicions and the presence of the Jack Pack on the nighttime streets. On that evening, however, I was lucky that both the cops and the Jack Dog would keep each other occupied as I went on the hunt for my number one tormenter. I wouldn't always be this lucky, so I had to make the best of it when I could.

Earlier I tried to subtly question Tish about the location of Dean's address. I never knew it myself – I was obviously never invited over, and

I was admittedly too afraid to enquire about it with anyone at school in the past. But Tish knew what it was since she was friends with his younger sister, Carrie, who now attended her school since Holy Apostate was closed down[3].

Yea, about that. I was acquainted with Carrie at Holy Apostate, and she was always very nice to me. She even defended me against her big brother on a few occasions. I was very grateful and appreciative of that, as not too many kids at that school were nice to me. I couldn't help wondering how it would affect her emotionally if I hurt and traumatized her brother. I felt a bona fide crisis in conscience developing.

I thought about it long and hard, and found myself bombarded by a montage of the numerous abusive things he did to me during those few years we shared a school building, including that time he pushed me down the stairs. So, what about *my* pain and trauma? He had always gotten off scot free, with no consequences. He needed to learn about the concept of consequences.

Those highly upsetting thoughts also riled the animal side that was now a part of me, and it hungered for blood. *His* blood. I began wondering if the animal side was always a part of me, and if the ritual simply brought it to the fore. Was I destined to never be a good person due to all the anger, bitterness, and hate stemming from my past abuse?

I put those uncomfy thoughts aside for the nonce and ultimately decided that Dean had it coming, and then some. And so, I approached Trish about the address.

"Why do you want to know where Carrie lives?" she wondered. "You never asked about it before."

"I'm just curious," I replied. "I'm wondering what school district that would put her in. After we had to leave Holy Apostate, its former students all ended up scattered around the city schools."

"Then I'll just tell you the district she's in."

"The address would help. It's not like I'm going to pay her a visit. We weren't *that* close, and you know I won't get within 500 feet of her brother's neighborhood. Besides, I get to hang with her when she comes here to see you anyways."

"Yea, okay."

---

[3] Yet another dramatic story for another time and place.

"He does still live with her, right?"

"Yea, why?"

"Well, I know their parents are divorced, and I was just curious again. So, what's the address?"

"Geez. They live over on Richmond."

"That's a long street, so you gotta be a bit more specific."

"You don't need to know more than that. I told you enough to figure out the school district, okay?"

*I'll have to work with what I could get out of her. I don't want to press her any further, since she's already getting suspicious. I can cover a lot of area quickly in wolfen form anyways.*

"Okay, so Carrie's school district would be Nativity. Thanks!"

"But you already knew they were going to Nativity!"

"Thanks!" I repeated before I sped off to prepare for the night's hunting.

***

As evening fell, I conducted the proper spell work, and within a minute I had morphed into lycan form. The Moon overhead was now moving into the waning phase, so I had less lunar energy to work with, but the change could still be done with a bit more effort.

I quickly rushed about the sprawling Richmond Avenue on all fours, darting in and out of alleys, backyards, and between parked vehicles. I managed to keep myself mostly unseen, except for one older lady walking her terrier that gasped as I dashed by them. Her dog also barked and whined furiously. I guessed another 'wolf man' sighting would soon be reported.

I figured that Dean would be out and about around the general area. I wasn't overly familiar with his out of school social habits, but it wasn't hard to figure out that a good-looking, athletic male teen would have a robust social life. He was a good student, but I doubted he went home too early based on the relatively little I knew about him outside of how much he loathed me and what a mean punch he had.

Another thing I didn't know at the time was that just a few blocks away, a largely abandoned tenement building on Prospect Avenue, used in the past by street gangs and drug dealers, had a new set of dangerous residents that attracted the attention of the police.

\*\*\*

Young officers Lamar Middleton and Ajay Phillips walked up to the dilapidated front door leading into the ground floor hallway with their hands on their gun holsters. The report said that a few screams were heard coming from within by people passing by, and the officers wanted to be cautious.

"Do you think the dealers moved back in?" Ajay asked his partner.

"Maybe," Lamar answered. "But do dealers usually scream?"

"If a deal goes wrong, possibly."

"Good point. Do you got your flashlight handy?"

"Of course, I do, man."

Ajay turned on his heavy flashlight and carefully pushed on the front door. It opened easily and he stepped in.

"Man, this place reeks like shit. As in, actual shit, mixed with piss. Someone, or something, must be living in here and using the floor as their john."

"Could it be people?"

"I dunno. Do bums or dealers usually shit and piss all over the floors?"

"You'd be surprised…"

Lamar suddenly heard a low growling coming from directly behind him. He turned to see a large, viciously snarling Siberian husky and what looked like an equally angry sheep dog beside it.

"Ajay, head's up!"

The two growling canines wasted no time in attacking Lamar. His police training served him well as he managed to draw his revolver and shoot the sheep dog through its right eye. As the wooly canine fell still, the husky managed to leap on the officer and knock him down, causing Lamar to drop his gun. The man did his best to grab the animal by its muzzle and hold it from getting its teeth into his throat.

Ajay brandished his firearm and pointed it at the struggle ensuing in front of him. "Lamar, strop struggling so much! I need to get a shot off, but I don't wanna risk hitting you instead of the animal!"

44

That was when Ajay heard another growling sound, this time coming from behind *him*. He swiftly turned to see two other snarling and slavering dogs emerge from empty apartment units on the first floor; they were both large and black, but it was too dark to discern the exact breeds. All that was important is that they both looked big, heavy, and nasty enough to rip a human being to shreds. The two aggressive animals stood close to each other, as if deliberately guarding something shrouded in the darkness behind them. The canine duo growled ferociously, and the officer could swear he saw eyeshine hovering more than five feet above the floor several feet behind them.

"Get back!" he shouted, hoping the animals would comprehend something of the danger they now faced.

As it turned out, what they comprehended well enough when they heard it was a challenge, and they ran towards Ajay growling and salivating with anticipation. The policeman shot the first one in the neck area before it could pounce on him. The dog screeched and fell to the filth-encrusted floor as a thin fountain of blood spewed from the wound. The second coal-furred canine managed to leap into the air towards its prey, but Ajay luckily got off another shot before that one could land on its target too. The bullet went clear through the dog's right shoulder blade while it was in mid-air.

The heavy canine's inertia was still enough to enable the large pouncing animal to knock the officer to the floor as it landed on him, however. Moreover, the dog was still alive despite being severely injured, and its wound had driven it into a blind rage.

Meanwhile, several feet away, Lamar struggled with his canine assailant by punching it several times in the muzzle. The animal was strong, but the officer was quite strong too and had years of boxing behind him. He knew he was still no physical match for a large, enraged husky, but he hoped to beat it back just enough so he could reach for his belt and grab his billy club. The determined officer finally managed this, though the dog clasped its powerful jaws on the wooden bludgeon as soon as the policeman revealed it.

"Son of a bitch!"

As for Ajay, the maddened black dog bit into his left arm as the patrolman moved the limb in front of his throat to block the attack. He screamed in pain as the canine's teeth sunk down through the skin of his forearm and raked the bone beneath. The officer struggled enough to retrieve his gun, which had landed on the floor next to him. He stuck the barrel into the side of the animal's furry neck and pulled the trigger. Ajay was sprayed by the canine's blood as the bullet penetrated clear through the animal's throat and dislodged its jaws from his arm.

The patrolman did his best to ignore the pain in his lacerated arm so he could kick the heavy corpse of the second dog off him and jump to his feet. It was then that the beast those first two ebony dogs were guarding emerged from the shadows of the inner corridor. Ajay gasped in horror at the sheer size and ugliness of the short-haired, reddish canine before him. Its eyes were almost white, and its bared teeth resembled the cutting implements of an Inquisition torturer.

"Oh, Jesus," he whispered to himself as the realization of what he was seeing fully sunk in. "The Jack Dog."

***

One thing that quickly amazed me about my new lupine form was how utterly tireless it was. I had rushed about the entirety of Richmond Avenue and surrounding neighborhoods numerous times in an hour, never skimping on the use of the instinctual stealth I now possessed to navigate the urban environment I was so familiar with. My lycanthropic predecessors may have called the forests their home, as did the actual wolves they patterned their animal forms after, but the 20th century was the era of a new environment characterized by concrete structures and metal conveyances. If one knew these environs well, and had the speed, strength, and stamina typical for one of Fenris' children, then all of that combined with the shroud of night made it relatively easy to avoid most human detection.

My visual and olfactory acuity scanned my surroundings as I navigated the streets at high speed, and I could identify no human scents familiar to me. Thankfully, I also caught no scent suggesting a group of canines that were clustered together – the latter being a threat I was concerned with. Of course, pedestrians were still out and about despite the danger presented by the pack, since the mayor was reluctant to declare a curfew at this point, and the Jack Dog was still considered "only" a legend despite the history of police run-ins with the monstrous red beast.

I had not yet acquired Dean's scent, so I had to rely on vision and the sound of his distinctive voice to spot him if he was wandering these streets. Within the hour, my single-minded persistence borne of the hunt had paid off. I clearly heard Dean's voice speaking to some people about three blocks distant. I rushed in that direction, ducking behind masonry, trees, and parked vehicles along the way. The closer I got, the more I realized there could be no doubt that the voice belonged to my hated quarry. I was quickly learning to hunt specific, targeted prey.

"So, are you gonna go out with her?" I heard an unfamiliar young male voice ask Dean as I hid behind the high brick stairway of a nearby house.

"I heard she's a good kisser, and gives hand jobs," another male voice said.

"Ha ha. We'll have to see," Dean replied. "I've been going with Jennifer since last month, and she would shit bricks if she found out."

I peeked out of my spot and had visual confirmation of what my pointed canine ears had told me: it was him, the worst tormentor of my life. And that was truly saying something. The sight of Dean O'Sullivan to go with the sound of his voice enraged me beyond description. Hence the prospect of holding back for even another full second was beyond my capabilities.

\*\*\*

Officer Lamar Middleton managed to whack the attacking husky with his billy club as it took another lunge at him. The dog yowled in pain and jumped back. It quickly shook off the blow, snarled in rage, and attacked again. It became obvious to the embattled lawman that this animal would not stop unless it was taken down for good. He thus stepped up the brutality of his counterattacks, swinging and smashing with the hardwood baton as aggressively as he could. The officer could hear the canine's facial and jaw bones cracking under each blow, and the blood trickling from its perked ears and darkened lips was a promising sign. Yet the beast kept on coming, so Lamar kept on smashing.

Just up the stairs and a few yards into the ground corridor the now panicked Officer Ajay Phillips pointed his gun towards the monstrous leader of the pack that was snarling at him. The Jack Dog seemed to recognize the threat of a firearm and jumped into the shadows to the right of the hallway with amazing speed and agility. The lawman let off a shot, but it sounded as if the bullet had hit something made of wood instead of flesh. The officer was trembling fiercely, and he knew his aim might be off, so he pooled his will and struggled to maintain control.

Ajay then heard his partner struggling with the snarling husky behind him. Still, he dared not turn his head and help the man who had recently become a valued friend. He shuddered and jumped back after he accidentally stepped on the bleeding corpse of one of the dogs he had shot to death. The officer was on edge and he had to keep as calm as possible to avoid making a fatal mistake.

The level of skill and courage Officer Ajay Phillips brought to bear under such pressure was nothing short of impressive. But this was the Jack Dog he was facing. The patrolman turned and fired to his left when he heard a sudden skittering in that direction. The shot was accompanied by the sound of shattering glass and it was evident he must have hit a discarded soda bottle that had been kicked over there. Then he heard a sudden snarl of rage and the loud pattering footsteps of the Jack Dog charging towards him.

The officer's reaction was swift, with his gun pointed in that direction and the trigger pulled in the blink of an eye… only to hear nothing but the click of an empty chamber. Had the Jack Dog actually counted the shots, or was it just a bizarre coincidence? Did it actually kick the glass bottle into the distance as a deliberate distraction to get the officer to waste a bullet, or was it just some random rat that happened to scamper over the glass container at just the "right" or "wrong" time (depending upon the Jack Dog's or Ajay's perspective, of course)?

Those disturbing questions regarding the level of this beast's cunning and intelligence were ultimately moot as the canine terror slammed into the officer with a force that seemed comparable to a stampeding bull. The dog's immense weight smashed Ajay against the wall, shattering the decaying stucco behind it and cracking several of the man's ribs. The lawman screamed as the huge red canine bit into his gut and tore out the man's bowels with a single swift move of its muscular neck.

Seconds earlier, Lamar finally succeeded in shattering the skull of the husky and severing one of its upper vertebrae after a final brutal blow with his nightstick. The dog whimpered pathetically yet attempted to take one last bite at him before it choked up a wad of blood and ceased further

48

movement. Still on an adrenal rush, the officer raised his baton and turned to his friend in the corridor. The sight of the Jack Dog holding the still twitching officer's intestines in its powerful jaws was a vision straight out of his worst nightmares.

"Ajay! Dear Jesus!"

Overcome by anger, Lamar swung his nightstick around in a menacing fashion.

"C'mon, mother fucker! *Come on!*"

The alpha canine spit the dying cop's pinkish guts from his mouth and snarled in anticipation of taking Lamar up on his challenge. The city had room for only one dominant, and this primal concern was all that mattered to the horror hound.

The fateful confrontation was interrupted as another cop car screeched to a stop in the street directly behind Lamar. Two other officers quickly disembarked from the vehicle and prepared to back up the first two lawmen on the scene. Lamar had no idea who had called for another car, but he was thankful that someone did.

"Lamar, what's going on up there?" he heard Officer Jude Lansky's familiar voice holler behind him.

The question was duly answered when the Jack Dog used that brief distraction to charge forward. He considered the two policemen with guns standing behind Lamar to be the greater threat. Hence, the monstrous canine simply barreled into the officer and knocked him down the small flight of stairs like a living steamroller. The huge red canine then charged at the other two patrolmen with incredible speed and leapt on Jude before he knew what was happening. The other officer, Doug Merval, shuddered in surprise and horror as he saw the Jack Dog rip into his partner and tear out the man's throat with a single horrific but efficient move.

Doug brandished his revolver, but the shock of what he had just witnessed caused him to hesitate for a critical second. That was all the time required by the Jack Dog to lunge and clamp his jaws around the wrist of the lawman's gun hand. Doug bellowed painfully and dropped the revolver as his radius and ulna were crushed into powder. The deranged canine then dragged the screaming officer up the street with surprising speed, as if to cunningly distance the man from his gun and to get out of range for when Lamar recovered and retrieved his own firearm.

"Merval!" he shouted as the strong young policeman jumped to his feet and picked up his revolver.

Lamar witnessed the Jack Dog dragging the 170-pound Doug Merval up the length of Prospect Avenue like a stuffed toy, leaving a trail of blood behind them. The patrolman pursued as quickly as he could on foot, all the while praying that Doug's weight would prevent the canine horror from moving too quickly. After running a block and a half, Lamar came across Doug laying in the middle of the street convulsing while making a few incoherent attempts to speak or scream.

"Merval! Are you okay, man?"

Lamar received his unfortunate answer when he reached the Doug's twitching body and noticed that his hand had been torn off the wrist and carried away. The fallen lawman was obviously but minutes away from bleeding out despite the makeshift tourniquet that Lamar hastily tied around his forearm in the hope of staunching the blood loss until EMTs could arrive.

The officer then stood up and turned frantically in every direction with his gun barrel pointed. The Jack Dog was nowhere in sight.

***

The bestial fury I experienced at the sight of Dean O'Sullivan for the first time in over a year boiled up and exploded like lava from an erupting volcano. I rushed out from the car I had hidden behind towards the target of my hunt and the source of so much of my past torment with the speed of a locomotive.

I leaped atop Dean and took him to the ground before he knew what hit him. I was certain I could hear at least two of his ribs splinter when he was brought down on the concrete under the weight of my massive furry form. In the process of my jump I side-smacked one of his two friends, knocking the athletic kid to the ground and forcing the wind out of his lungs. He continued to lay there stunned for the duration.

"Holy shit!" the still standing friend yelled at the sight before him.

Dean was beyond being simply stunned as he lay under the crushing weight of my huge furry form while gasping for air. I then rose into a bipedal stance, giving him a clear look at the raging beast now tearing into him; a beast that, as far as I was concerned, was partly his creation. *He* had unleashed this monster on the world. *He* had made me want to become what I now was. And *he* would pay for that, in gory spades.

"Dean!" the still standing boy yelled.

The latter teen's build and stance made it clear he was a football player, likely a member of the school team that Dean probably also belonged to. The young jock rushed at the beast towering before him (i.e., yours truly) to help his friend. My response was to swing my arm and backhand him. Like a fly hit by a swatter the athlete was sent through the air to land almost twenty feet away on the pavement by the curb. He, too, was out for the duration with the wind knocked out of him The level of strength I had in this form was amazing.

I then reached down, grabbed Dean by his thick jacket, and hoisted him into the air as if he were a stuffed animal. I slammed him up against the brick wall of a nearby apartment building. Then I snarled in his face, baring my teeth and preparing to literally tear his face off.

"Stop! Don't..." was all he could say as blood dribbled out of his nose and mouth.

I tried forcing myself to speak comprehensible words as another montage of Dean's past abuse cascaded across my psyche. I was only partly successful.

"You... hurt me! Now I hurt... *back!*"

I then raked Dean across the chest, my talons easily ripping through his jacket, the shirt underneath that, and the flesh beneath the cloth. He let out an agonized scream as blood poured out of the four deep slash wounds now ripped into his upper torso. The smell of the blood pushed my animal side into a frenzy. My human side could only smell the even sweeter scent of bitter vengeance.

*Yes!*

A memory then flew through my mind, one of Dean punching me in the stomach and then driving his knee into my balls while yelling, "You asshole!"

I slammed him up against the wall again as I forced a few more words through my non-human larynx: *"You...ass-hol-lllee...!"*

Then I opened my jaws again and moved to rip off the handsome features that were the envy of the boys at Nativity and formerly Holy Apostate School, the latter of which included me.

Then other images cascaded through my mind. They were recollections of the kind words of his younger sister. Another was of the kindness shown to me by his grandmother who I once chanced to meet while walking with Carrie. It was thoughts of what my actions would do to them. The animal inside me wanted blood, and so did the human part of me. The two sides of my psych were actually in accord on this. But another aspect of my human side vied with them. I snarled in rage as the battle continued for close to a minute but seeming like an eternity.

I then heard police sirens coming from several blocks away. They were obviously heading in my direction and I estimated they would be there in about twenty seconds. Someone had obviously seen this play out from their front window and promptly called the police.

*No… more…*

I hurled Dean's limp and injured form several yards away, and he thumped down on a large island of grass. The evening hunt completed, I turned and rushed down Richmond Avenue in the opposite direction from which the police cars were fast approaching. I was out of the area within seconds.

***

The next morning found me walking in the brisk October air up Prospect Avenue towards the large library located in Downtown Buffalo. It was my intention to conduct some research on the occult and local legends there. I elected to walk rather than take a bus, as I wanted to clear my head and avoid conflicts with potential troublemakers that plagued the public transportation system. I simply had to do something to make productive use of the time that became available to me due to my suspension.

I hadn't bothered to watch the morning news for the report on Dean getting slashed up. I didn't want to risk seeing images of his crying family members being interviewed. I still hated him beyond measure, not only for hurting me but for making me want to unleash the beast I had now become on him in the first place. I finally got the revenge I had so often daydreamed about over the past year, yet I didn't know how I felt about it. There was more to the situation than I had imagined, and I was conflicted.

These thoughts filled my head as I approached the driveway of a certain house. No one else seemed out and about this early in the morning. No one human, that is (other than me, if I still counted as such.) Suddenly standing before me were the growling forms of two large dogs, a Siberian husky and a German shepherd, having exited from the backyard of the house directly in front of me. They were clearly members of the Jack Pack, as I called it, and they were out for blood.

*Seriously? In the middle of the day? I thought they only attacked at night!* The situation with the pack was obviously escalating to a new level. *And... I'm in my human form. I don't know if I can change in the day at all!*

I reached down into my pocket and drew the switchblade I had purchased from the Japanese shop located within the Main Center Mall to use in self-defense when I was stuck in human form. I couldn't bring it to school, but I learned to carry it around with me while out and about in the city. I hit the tiny side lever that extended the sharp blade and pointed it at the two snarling dogs.

"Get back! Or do you want some of this?"

The terror I initially felt was soon taken over by the animal side, which could assert itself even when I was in human form if I found myself threatened or under undue stress. I was prepared to fight for my life with nothing more than a blade backed by adrenaline and a dash of animal fury, and it would be interesting to see how I could handle myself like this. The dogs growled and moved closer, clearly not intimidated, and eager to answer the challenge.

The husky attacked first, but it whined and backed off after I sliced it across the muzzle. The German shepherd used the distraction to move in and bite my leg, tearing at the bottom of my jeans. As I moved to stab at it, the husky rushed forward with another attack. It backed away again when I slashed the blade at its face, but the shepherd was still pulling at my leg, determined to wrench me off my feet. The husky's lunges made certain I didn't have time to stab the other dog in the neck or the eyes. I was clearly in some deep shit, vulnerable in my human form.

As it turned out, however, I would not be fighting alone. A middle-aged man, a lean African American fellow with a cane, turned the nearby corner just in time to see my plight. He hurried to my aid, with his walking stick raised as a weapon.

"Those goddamned dogs! Attacking people in the daytime now! Get away from that kid!"

The man ran to my side and struck the German shepherd on the neck with two quick swipes of the cane. He was obviously used to using it in self-defense. The snarling canine released my leg and turned its attention to my helper as I continued to hold off the husky with a series of jabs and slashes from my blade, one of which left a crimson stain on the white fur of its left shoulder.

The German shepherd furiously charged my helper, who beat it back with several strong blows of his wooden stick. The dog seemed to realize it would not be able to get a good bite in without being clobbered, so it backed away and retreated to the front of the yard it first emerged from with the other one, as if to contemplate a new strategy of attack. The husky found itself in the same situation as it came to learn that the bite of my blade was as bad as the one it could deliver with its teeth. It too turned and dashed to the side of its fellow attacking canine. These dogs had a clear pack mentality fueled by an uncanny level of cooperation.

My helper then ran to my side. "Kid, are you alright?"

"Yea, and thank you. I'm Mike, by the way."

"I'm Everett," he answered. "And it's no problem. Those goddamned dogs attacking people! They think they own the streets now. They're as bad as those gangs were before that guy in the bird mask drove them off."[4]

Our respite was short-lived, however. We heard more growling as two rottweilers emerged from another yard two houses down on the opposite side of the block. They were quickly joined by a viciously snarling Doberman pincher and a bull terrier that appeared out of some bushes to join the husky and German shepherd duo that had already attacked us.

"Shit," we both said simultaneously.

Yea, Everett and I were totally in the deepest shit imaginable now. As if I really needed to point that out.

Another brief distraction, this time a welcome one, ensued when an elderly woman across the street opened her front door to retrieve her morning paper. She noticed the situation going on in the street and a look of horror came over her features.

---

[4] Who the hell is the darkly-clad vigilante in the bird mask who *ravaged* gang bangers and the rest of the criminal element in the Queen City during the 1980s? Nero will meet him in Book 4… and will quickly wish he hadn't!

"Ma'am, call the cops!" Everett yelled. "And stay inside!"

The lady frantically nodded her head and darted back into her home, slamming the door shut behind her. How long would it take the fuzz to arrive, though?

Everett then turned to me as the dogs prepared to pounce as a group. "Kid, run up on one of the porches and try to hide! I'll do the best I can to hold 'em off 'till the cops get here! Go!"

*This stranger is going to risk himself for me? I… have to try to change into the wolf.* Now. *In the daytime. I'm going to kill these fucking mutts, and I mean all of them, once and for all! But I can't do it as a human!*

I gritted my teeth as the animal rage and determination to survive and prove myself the dominant alpha of the city bubbled to the surface.

Everett pushed me away as hard as he could. "Go, kid! Now!"

The dogs chose that moment to attack. Everett raised his cane and swung it around in wide circling arcs, both to draw the pack's attention away from me and to hold them at bay for as long as he could. I did indeed dash away, but not to one of the porches. I instead rushed towards a nearby parked van and crawled under it, hoping to evade the dogs that came at me for a minute or two. I then began concentrating hard on an image of the full moon and calling upon Fenris. *I need your power, and I need it now, Great One! In the daylight! Let me absorb whatever remnants of the lunar light may remain from the previous night! I beseech thee for thy aid!*

The husky and shepherd involved in the initial attack resumed their two-prong assault and struggled to slide under the vehicle to get at me, chomping and snarling at my extremities. I swiped the knife at them to keep them back to the best of my ability while desperately calling out to Fenris and pouring every iota of emotion I had into the image of the full moon. The dogs would periodically whine and retreat several inches when I managed to slice their skin with the blade, but they still kept on trying to sink their teeth into me despite the risk of getting cut by my knife again. And due to the awkward position I was in, I was not able to inflict anything worse than superficial cuts on them.

In the meantime, Everett fought valiantly against the attacking rottweilers, Doberman, and terrier with his cane. He was a tough and determined older guy who managed to smack the terrier into unconsciousness and a broken jaw within moments. But there was no way he was taking down those rottweilers, or even the Doberman when it was

55

backed up by the latter two. The courageous man could only shout in pain and swear in frustration while continuing to beat one of the rottweilers away as the Doberman bit into his left leg and the other rottweiler clasped its vice-like jaws onto his free arm.

Just across the street the husky and shepherd were undaunted by the swipes of my blade and continued to advance underneath the vehicle... until they were abruptly pulled all the way under. No human screams could be heard, but only the sounds of fearsome growls followed by the high-pitched cries of dogs in pain. A pool of blood seeped out from under the vehicle, and most of it wasn't mine.

A moment later, the car was lifted up as a werewolf emerged from under it on two legs. A loud crashing sound was heard as I released the vehicle upon walking out from beneath it. Being a lycanthrope in the daylight was at first disconcerting, but the animal and human side of my psyche combined into a sort of harmonious fusion upon seeing brave old Everett finally pulled to the ground by the rottweiler and Doberman that had seized his limbs. The other rottweiler was now freed from being struck by the cane, and it jumped on top of the man to tear out his throat and feed on his entrails.

"You goddamned bitches! You goddamned... huh?"

The injured Everett was startled as the rottweiler that jumped on him was suddenly lifted into the air before it could do any serious damage to the man. Now possessing the power of the lycanthrope, I grabbed the dog in a rib-crushing pincer hold I had learned in my childhood while I sunk my teeth into its throat. I ripped out the canine's trachea and hurled its corpse aside.

I then clutched the remaining rottweiler and Doberman by the throats and yanked them off Everett. I tossed them several yards away with a surge of strength that no normal human could match. The man looked up at the gray-furred beast before him and at first took on an expression of horror.

"Oh, shit. There goes the neighborhood..." he lamented while preparing to die horribly a moment later.

That's not what happened, however. Much to his surprise, the werewolf (that was me!) lifted Everett off the asphalt and tossed up him up onto the roof of a tall 1975 Ford Econoline van that was parked directly behind us. It would now be very difficult for the dogs to get at the man.

With this done, I crouched down and roared a challenge to the snarling dogs as I allowed my animal side to take over completely.

"Is that the wolf man people been seein'? And he's... helping me?" Everett said aloud to himself incredulously.

The Doberman rushed at me a bit sooner than the remaining rottweiler did, and I stayed on two legs as I bashed each side of its head with my enormous fists as it leapt at my throat. My enhanced hearing duly noted the animal's skull and everything inside it being crushed like a melon. The dog fell to the asphalt at my canine feet and I prepared myself for the rottweiler's attack. I knew that one was going to be more difficult.

I understood that I had to prevent its jaws from getting a grip on one of my limbs, let alone my throat. I was too tall in werewolf form for a throat attack to happen as easily as it could in my human form, but my extremities were just as vulnerable. So, I decided to use the human cunning I had but the dog lacked to my advantage when it rushed at me.

Just before it could reach one of my legs I slumped down on all fours and caught its neck in my muzzle. I sunk my razor-sharp teeth deep into its throat, lifted it into the air on two legs, and violently shook the animal around until I heard and felt its upper vertebrae snap like a twig. I then simply spit the bloody canine corpse onto the street.

"Well, I'll be a son of a bitch..." Everett said quietly to himself as he witnessed the events from atop the Econoline.

That was when the police cars finally arrived; two of them, in fact. The vehicles with the flashing lights screeched to a halt several feet from me, and two cops emerged from the first car with their guns in hand. One of them, I would later learn, was Lamar Middleton. Needless to say, the barrels of their revolvers were aimed in my direction the second they caught sight of the werewolf standing before them.

"It's the wolf man!" Lamar shouted, as if that wasn't obvious. "It must have killed those dogs in some type of territorial dispute, or something."

"Well, shoot the damn thing!" his new partner, Renny, yelled.

I snarled at them angrily as I prepared to see how well this body took ordinary lead bullets, as there would be no way to completely dodge the impending fusillade.

"No, wait!" Everett shouted from atop the van. "Don't shoot the wolf man. He – I think it's a 'he,' anyways – helped me when the dogs attacked!"

"Are you serious?" Lamar replied. "And how the hell did you get up there?"

"I'm dead serious!" Everett replied. "And I'd be only 'dead' if not for that wolf! He put me up here to keep me safe from those goddamned dogs while he whaled on 'em!"

The two officers from the second cop car then disembarked.

"Oh, what the fuck?" one of them, Boyd, exclaimed when he saw me in my full hirsute and snarling glory. "Is that... *him?*"

"Should we open fire?" the final cop, Starsky, queried. "I mean, it's gotta be part of that dog pack! Maybe the alpha of the pack, too!"

"No!" Everett shouted. "He's not with the dogs! He saved me from them!"

"Who the hell is that guy up on the van's roof?" Starsky asked his partner, Boyd.

Lamar wanted to open fire, and really believed that he should, remembering what happened to poor Ajay, his previous partner during their recent confrontation with the Jack Pack. He kept his gun trained on me, and my bright yellow eyes were focused on him as my animal side was enraged by the threat. *Could I get that gun from him before he can shoot? Maybe lop off his hand?*

Before either of us could make a decision, however, the shit hit the fan in a major way. In an unbelievable way, really.

All present at the time were startled when Starsky suddenly screamed as another rottweiler jumped on him from behind and bit into his neck. Almost all the blood in his body emptied onto the streets as the vicious canine punctured the man's jugular.

"Shit!" Boyd yelled as he drew his revolver and shot the dog twice in the side.

No sooner was that animal killed than another German shepherd and Doberman dashed from seemingly out of nowhere and pounced on Boyd. He screamed bloody hell as the first dog literally bit his nose off and the second ripped open his testicles. Believe me, I really wish I had made that one up.

*Shit! Did they know enough to approach downwind? I didn't catch their scent before they attacked! Am I even at full capacity in the daylight?*

Lamar and Renny turned and opened fire on the canine duo in unison. The attacking beasts were riddled with two bullets each, and their seeping blood joined Boyd's and Starsky's in staining the asphalt bright red.

I now wondered if I should give into my bestial side and tear into Lamar and Renny from behind before they could turn their guns back on me. The animal persona I shared this form with practically begged for me to do it.

*So, should I? Or…?*

"Wolf dude, look out!" Everett hollered from atop the van.

The warning helped me turn just in time as another Doberman sneakily emerged from beneath a bush and leapt at my throat. I caught the animal in my superhumanly strong hands and slammed its skull hard against the street. Need I mention it was out of the fight?

That is when I caught the scent of more approaching dogs (these ones were not downwind), as well as hearing the staccato thumping of their heartbeats. I heard still more from the other direction, as Lamar and Renny turned to see four additional dogs emerge from the backyards adjacent to the various houses on the block. Two rottweilers, a Siberian husky, and a pit bull now confronted the remaining two policemen.

"Oh, Jesus, Middleton," Renny said nervously. "I dunno if we have enough bullets for this."

"Stay firm, man," Lamar replied. "When your chamber goes empty, drop the gun and draw your baton as fast as you can. Let's take as many as we can with us. Let's make those mother fuckers work for this one."

What suddenly appeared in my direction was even more extraordinary, though. A rottweiler and a German shepherd emerged from around the corner and faced off against me, while striding several feet behind them was nothing less than the Jack Dog himself. This was obviously a "do or die moment" for the leader of the pack. Seeing the red-furred beast in the full light was enough to make even a werewolf wince in fear. Which it did. But I wasn't as scared as I was thoroughly pissed off since my animal side's desire to kill and dominate rose like a thermometer's mercury on a blazing summer day.

The four dogs facing the two cops rushed out in side directions, as if trying to confuse the policemen and make it more difficult to draw a bead on them. That seemed to work, as the first shot fired by Renny missed its target. The best jumper among them, the husky, actually managed to catch

Everett's scent despite his location atop the van and it attempted to leap up onto the roof of the tall vehicle. It only managed to land on the front windshield, but it struggled to scamper up the slick glass to reach the top of the van. Just as the vicious dog's fluffy white head and front legs made it over the side of the vehicle's roof Everette punched it hard in the snout. The animal lost its traction and slipped back down onto the street.

"Goddamned dogs!" the man yelled.

As the husky landed on the street, its skull became the recipient of a more successful bullet from Renny's gun. The officer then turned and looked around for the other attacking dogs, but apparently all of them had taken refuge behind parked vehicles or bushes. Lamar was eye scanning the vicinity in the same way, turning in a circle with his revolver drawn, waiting for one of the dogs to emerge from somewhere.

Over on my end one of the rottweilers charged at me while snarling like the mad dog it was. I did the same in return and I slashed at its face as it leapt at me. I managed to tear out one of its eyes, but the furry beast weathered the pain and continued barking and snarling at me. Then the other one attacked as I was distracted. I heard the patter of its paws on the asphalt as it did so, and I quickly turned and sliced open its belly with my claws while it was in mid-leap. The animal landed on the street with a loud thwapping sound, its guts spilling out onto the street beside it.

Unfortunately, its partner with the missing eye used this split second to move in and clasp its powerful jaws onto my left leg. I yelped in pain as the Jack Dog, the ringmaster of this slaughter fest, began moving in closer.

Meanwhile, Lamar and Renny both turned to their left when they heard a snarl from that direction. It had apparently come as a distraction from a dog in hiding, since as soon as the officers looked around one of the rottweilers rushed out from behind a car and leaped on Renny. It took him straight to the ground, and Lamar turned and shot the dog through the jaw. The impact sent it rolling off his partner while also spraying the officer's face and upper torso with what looked like half a gallon of animal blood.

That particular distraction was all the pit bull needed to slide out from under a car on the other side of the street to charge at and lock its jaws onto Lamar's gun wrist. He dropped the weapon and released a pain-wracked shout as the small but powerful dog pulled him down onto the street, away from the revolver. Renny reached for his own gun to return

60

the favor to his partner only to find three of his four fingers taken into the mouth of the last remaining rottweiler before he could grip the weapon. The lawman shrieked as the dog tore the four digitals clean off his hand.

As in his previous encounter, Lamar managed to get his billy club from its belt holder and to furiously beat the pit bull with it. The dog maintained its lock on his wrist despite the brutal assault the officer inflicted upon the animal with his baton, and the policeman could feel his carpal bones begin to break. The officer was nothing if not persistent, however, and his own adrenal-fueled anger allowed him to fracture the animal's skull with a final powerful strike from his club. The pit bull then ceased moving with its jaws still locked onto the cop's wrist. Lamar then used the end of his nightstick to pry open the dead animal's mouth.

Unfortunately, the rottweiler that divested Renny of his fingers saw this and rushed at Lamar, who would be completely unprepared for the coming attack.

"No!" Renny bellowed as he reached out his intact hand and grasped the dog's tail with all the strength he could muster (luckily, the animal had never had its tail docked).

Furious at having its attack halted, the dog turned on Renny again. The officer screamed as the animal jumped on him and bit into his face.

Lamar responded by hurling his club at the dog with his good hand.

The rottweiler yelped in pain and was dislodged from Renny's face as the wooden stick struck it hard on the side of its head. While the dog was still dazed Lamar pushed past the pain of his broken wrist as he ran for his gun where it lay several feet distant. He managed to grab it just as the rottweiler shook off the effects of the cop's blow and ran at him growling. The officer reached the gun, turned towards the attacking canine, and fired the weapon. The bullet entered the animal's gaping maw and exited out the lower portion of its skull.

With the final dog on their side of the block taken down, Lamar ran over to his fallen comrade, expecting to see the worst. What he saw certainly wasn't good, as Renny had a brutal facial wound in addition to a hand now missing four fingers. He was alive and conscious, however.

"Did you…?"

"Yeah, I got the bastard, Renny. Now lay back, don't try to move or talk, and I'll call for help."

"But… the werewolf…?"

"I guess I'll have to deal with that first. Just hold tight, okay? I'll get you help."

A few minutes before that, I had responded to the sole remaining rottweiler biting into my leg by grasping its jaws in my hands and pulling both ends of its chops apart with all my superhuman might. I pried the dog's mouth open and kept pulling until its entire jawbone broke with a loud cracking sound. The animal fell still with a copious amount of blood seeping out of its now freakishly wide mouth.

I then turned my attention towards the slowly approaching Jack Dog. I wasn't hurt too badly, as I managed to get the rottweiler off me before it could do any serious damage. I was fit for a major fight. But this would be the biggest fight of my early "career" as a werewolf. I mean, this was the Jack Dog here.

I didn't care, however. My rage was burning white hot, and I snarled a challenge at the huge abomination of a canine standing proudly on all fours before me. The Jack Dog snarled in return as if saying, "Let's do this, fucker!"

I eagerly complied and we clashed like a couple of fur-covered juggernauts. We bit and tore at each other in a hellish frenzy as we rolled across the early morning street, neither of us giving the other a single quarter or hint of mercy. My animal side was completely in control, and it was thoroughly enjoying this battle no matter how much blood and flesh I lost.

"Holy shit!" Everett said from his vantage point atop the van. "Is that... the Jack Dog that the wolf dude is fighting? Is he behind the pack of dogs? And ain't he supposed to be dead?"

Lamar rushed to his car and called for major back-up and an ambulance on the dispatch. He then ran towards the scene of the final battle, his gun pointed with its two remaining bullets searching for a target.

"Officer, don't shoot!" Everett yelled. "Y'all might hit the wolf man! I think he's on our side! I think that other one's the Jack Dog come back to life or somethin'!"

"Both of them have to be stopped!" the lawman insisted.

"No, man, try to hit only the Jack Dog if ya can!"

Speaking of which, I hurled the monstrous red canine off me, but he sprung back on powerful legs and took me right down under the force of his charge. His strength was immense, and his speed was just as incredible. This was no ordinary mean and ferocious dog, but the product of something beyond the pale. I raked him with my talons as he attacked, and the Jack Dog backed away with several tears marring his flesh. Rather than stop, however, he growled and rushed at me again. I slashed at him only to see the beast jump to the side to evade my talons. He then leaped at me again and managed to latch onto my neck. The reddish beast used the firm hold he had to pull me to the ground with minimal effort.

I backhanded him before he could fully sink those horrid teeth into my throat. The force sent him sliding back but he still appeared to be just barely stunned by my strongest blow. The beast didn't succeed in ripping out my throat, but he had briefly gotten his teeth into it, and I was seriously hurting. The drops of blood that continually dripped down from my wounded neck to leave numerous scarlet mini-puddles on the street beneath me made that as clear as a search light illuminating the nighttime sky.

The Jack Dog then emitted a truly terrifying growl as he ran towards me again at high speed, as if determined to end this once and for all. He slammed into me with what felt like the power of a speeding semi-truck, which sent me sprawling into the door of a nearby parked car so hard that the metal caved in and the side window shattered. I struck back with two powerful hits to the monster animal's jaw, then ripped into the flesh on top of his head. The creature yelped as blood spurted from his torn scalp.

I followed that up by kicking him in the collarbone. This sent the beast sliding back across the street. However, as he always seemed to do, the Jack Dog shook off the pain and bared his teeth with another vicious growl as he prepared to tear into me again.

I stood in a crouching position and snarled back, at the same time moving my human-shaped arms in a beckoning gesture to let him know I was ready and waiting for the next attack.

*Let's do this, asshole!*

That is when two other cop cars screeched into view, as Lamar's back-up had finally arrived. The Jack Dog didn't fail to notice this. In a really slick move, he turned his attention from me to the lead cop car and ran towards it with speed reminiscent of a freight train.

The monster canine leapt what must have been more than fifteen feet over the trunk of the vehicle so that a combo of the dog's inertia and pulverizing strength carried his ugly head clear through the windshield.

The cop on the driver's side shrieked as the dog ignored the shards of glass embedded in his bloodied face and tore off the officer's nose and lips in a single chomp.

The officer on the driver's side jumped out of the car and shot at the Jack Dog. The animal was hit in the side, but despite the bloody wound and a yelp of pain the red-furred beast remained standing. He jumped off the hood in a blur of motion before the cop could fire again, slamming into the lawman and taking him right to the ground. It was as horrifying to hear the officer's death screams as it was to witness the enraged Jack Dog biting into the man's throat with such jaw-crushing force that his head was nearly severed.

"Shit!" Lamar yelled as he aimed his revolver and shot the Jack Dog on the other side of his body.

The animal again howled in pain yet still remained on his feet. The Jack Dog's mouth was dripping with the blood and chunks of esophagus from the cop he killed as the murderous canine growled in defiance at Lamar and rushed at him. The beast's wounds slowed him down just enough so that the officer was able to shoot the monster canine in the shoulder with his last bullet.

The Jack Dog was stopped cold, but just shook his head and growled despite the blood pouring out of so many gaping wounds. Just then the two cops in the other car both disembarked from their vehicle and emptied their magazines into the animal. The alpha canine then finally fell, but it continued to snarl and twitch about as if its bloodlust was still not sated. I looked on from a distance as the three remaining cops brandished their batons and began beating what life remained out of the creature.

As this went on, Everett pointed at me from atop the van and yelled, "Go! Go!"

I took his good advice and rushed into a nearby yard, pushing through the pain of my rapidly healing wounds while making a clean getaway.

# EPILOGUES

Within the hour a reporter from Eyewitness News was interviewing Lamar and Everett on the street where the battle had taken place. The former was standing with his broken wrist bandaged up. The more seriously but not fatally injured older man was laying on a wheeled stretcher, the terrible wounds on two limbs and the front of his chest wrapped in bandages, as he awaited the EMTs on the scene to bring him to an ambulance following the interview he agreed to give.

"So, Officer Middleton, do you think the threat to the city presented by this pack of feral dogs is over now?" Kathleen Evans asked.

"I can't say for certain," Lamar replied, "but I think so. We got the pack leader, so I believe it's likely that this is over. We are, of course, going to request 24-hour patrols over the next few weeks just to make certain."

"Okay, good," Kathleen said. "You seem to have sustained an injury to your wrist, as it's swathed in bloody bandages. Are you all right?"

"The EMTs wouldn't have let me stay on the scene for this interview if it was life-threatening. I'll get it fully treated right after this."

"And your partner, Renny McClaine?" she continued. "We heard he was one of the surviving officers but was very seriously injured."

"His injuries were much more severe than mine, yes. But if I know Renny, he'll pull through just fine. I was lucky to have him at my side today. The man is a true hero."

Kathleen smiled. "Yes, it seems you men with the badges are all true heroes."

"Thank you, Kathleen, though a badge isn't required to make a hero, as Everett proved today."

"The wolf man is a hero too!" Everett interjected.

"Excuse me, Mr. ...?" the reporter said as she shifted the mic over to the face of the new speaker.

Lamar sighed noticeably.

"Everett Williams here. I gotta say that while the cops shot down the Jack Dog in the end, the wolf man helped with the whole thing and even went one-on-one with it for a while. He saved my life. I know reports say he's been attacking folks, but I don't think he's all bad. Not totally. He might just have some issues with some folks. We don't know all there is to know about him yet."

"Oh, really?" Kathleen replied before turning back to Lamar. "Officer, did you see this reputed wolf man on the scene?"

"Is she sayin' I might be a liar?" Everett queried with annoyance.

"No, no, Everett," Lamar stated firmly. "Calm down there. I think Kathleen is just wondering if I agree that what we saw was really a werewolf. And I can't really say that it was."

"It done looked like a werewolf to me, man!" Everett insisted.

"And you have seen enough werewolves in your time to know one when you see one, Mr. Williams?" Kathleen asked with a smirk.

"I done saw me enough movies to know one when I see one!" Everett spat back. "And I don't think he's all bad."

"Okay, gentlemen, that's enough for now," Kathleen said to end the interview. "I thank you both for your time, I wish you both a speedy recovery, and God bless both of you for getting through this. It's good to know we have heroes we can count on when a crisis appears, both with and without badges."

"Yup. Some of them even wear shaggy coats," Everett said aloud after the on the scene newscaster had walked away.

The older man then turned his head to Lamar's direction and asked, "You know that was a werewolf, am I right, Officer?"

"Everett, I'm not the only one with some injuries that need to be tended to. Let the EMTs bring you to the hospital now, alright?"

"Sure. You went and gave me my answer by changing the subject anyways."

As the EMTs were about to cart Everett to the waiting ambulance, Lamar reached out and halted them.

"Sorry, but one more quick question for Mr. Williams," the lawman said. "Everett, if that was a werewolf we saw – and I'm not saying that it was – well, it's been said they have a human form. According to the stories, anyways. Since you were the first on the scene, do you have any idea who this werewolf might actually be? *If* that's what it was, of course."

"No, sir," Everett replied. "I don't got the foggiest."

As the EMTs carried him towards the waiting ambulance, the older man looked at the tattered remains of the jacket and jeans blowing about in the October wind that he recognized as the clothing worn by the young man he had met and helped during the early part of the fracas. *Don't you worry none, young Mike. I won't say a word. In fact, I hope we meet again one day.*

***

Luckily, I had managed to get indoors during the day without the people I lived with seeing me go in the back door wearing nothing except my trusty stretchable gym shorts. I was still going to need an explanation for my mother as to why I was now minus a coat and a pair of jeans, though.

It was also much more difficult sneaking around during the daytime, which is another reason I elected not to make a habit of doing daytime transformations. I also felt seriously weak after changing back to human, and it lasted over an hour. Without the benefit of the direct energies from a full or at least waxing moon, I now knew that making the change under less than ideal conditions was something to reserve for emergencies only. I still hadn't figured out exactly how the shamanistic werewolf thing worked; if it was the same for all of us, if it evolved with time and practice, etc. There was far too much to know about this topic to get all the info from either the scroll Rutger gave me or the few books I managed to find on the topic thus far. Trial and error was obviously going to be part of the deal.

All I did know at the time as I laid there in bed resting off the remnants of the post-day transformation weakness was that there were many more things I could accomplish with that power. This included more people whom I owed some payback to, and I knew there were doubtless others I had yet to meet who would cross me and require a lesson that only the werewolf could provide.

Not only that, but the problems stemming from the family that Fate had saddled me with was another issue I would have to contend with, not to mention them, my friends, and fellow students figuring things out. Of equal concern, I knew, were the other types of paranormal or strange events and entities that would pop up around here which might prove to be a challenge even for the power of the werewolf. Then there were the police that now knew about me, particularly Lamar Middleton. Finally, there was the "payment" I now owed to the Brotherhood of Fenris coming due somewhere down the line.

I had no idea what the future would bring, but it was more than enough to know that the hunt was on, and I was ecstatic. If only I had known in those halcyon days what was in store for me...

\*\*\*

Several blocks away from Mike Nero, a strange man and woman exited an apartment building. It was the first time they had been outside in months. They appeared to be in their sixties and had resided close to Nero during his childhood. This mysterious, seldom seen couple were expert dog breeders, as well as being much more than that.

"We finally managed to breed another one," the woman said in frustration, "and then this one had to get away too. Look at the problems it ended up causing for the city. How many dead this time? We never expected our baby to bring a whole pack of dogs together under his control."

"A lot about this project of ours yielded unexpected results," the man responded. "Do not worry, we will get it right eventually."

"We will? I am sure you must realize the gap of time it took us to breed the second one after we lost the first. It will likely require a similar span of years before we could manage to bring forth a third. And these are years we may not have left to us, dear."

"Oh, I would not be too quick to jump to that conclusion. I suspect nature may have its own way of helping us along. Now that the pack is taken care of, and it is safe to come out again, we just need to keep looking around in case the 'call of the wild' has saved us the trouble of having to take matters into our own hands."

Later that very evening, a simple event occurring in the cellar of an abandoned ramshackle home on the Lower West Side would prove the man correct. A female pooch yowled in pain as she gave birth to a new litter. The first few puppies to leave the womb presented no problems; it was the final and biggest one that was proving an issue for the new canine mom. She nevertheless pushed as hard as she could, and the pain ended as she finally forced out a more unusual puppy. This one was larger than the rest, with a short coat of reddish fur and cries that sounded deeper and more grotesque than those of its siblings.

**END**

**Publisher's note:** Thank you for reading, and I hope you liked the first entry in the Nero saga, and if you did like what you read, please do not hesitate to mention this via reviews on Amazon, Goodreads, your personal blogs, and anywhere else that reviews of horror fiction (or books in general) are welcome! The more reviews we get, the more books we will sell; and the more we sell, the more projects we can bring to fruition for our readers!

The paperback for *Nero Book 2: The Mummy Strikes* will be coming soon! Additionally, you will get to see more of Mike Nero in stories taking place in more recent years up to the present in other publications from Wild Hunt Press, including our upcoming continuing prose horror anthologies *Boogey Knights* and *Mansion of the Macabre,* along with various other projects we are planning! Visit the Wild Hunt Press page and public group on Facebook for announcements and discussions on how to make our publications the best they can be for you, our readers.

# ABOUT THE AUTHOR

Christofer Nigro is a life-long fan of fantastic fiction that spans the genres from horror, sci-fi, fantasy, super-heroes, kaiju/tokusatsu, pulp adventure, crime noir, steampunk, you name it. He has had novels published by Severed Press and short stories published in anthologies from Black Coat Press, Pro Se Press, Sirens Call Publications, Grinning Skull Press, Pulp Empire, Horrified Press, and the Kaiju Vs. Cancer charity label. In 2018 he established his own small publishing outfit, Wild Hunt Press, to bring you affordable and cutting edge prose material in the above genres – but particularly in horror and kaiju – from both himself and many other authors, both new and established. He now works feverishly on running this label full time and as a freelance editor.